The
Dark

Canoe

Other Books by SCOTT O'DELL

The
Dark
Canoe

SCOTT O'DELL

Illustrated by Milton Johnson

HOUGHTON MIFFLIN COMPANY BOSTON

"Oh! Ahab," cried Starbuck,
"not too late is it, even now . . .
See! Moby Dick seeks thee not.
It is thou, thou, that madly
seekest him!"

Herman Melville

The
Dark
Canoe

1

I⊤ CAME floating up to us at dusk without a sound, on
the running tide, through more than five fathoms of
murky water, out of the heart of Magdalena Bay.

There was no breeze on that day in September. No
leaf turned among the mangroves. Not a fish leaped
nor a wing stirred anywhere. And to the north of
where our ship lay anchored, the salt marshes glittered
as if they were on fire.

Yet there were two men in our crew who said they
had sailed into ports where the sun was so hot that the
waters steamed and boiled. Jim Blanton said that he
knew a place where the sun never set, but shone night
and day. And Judd, the carpenter, swore with a hand
clasped to his heart that once in the Strait of Madagas-
car he had cooked his supper on the iron fluke of a

1

ship's anchor. I still think that the sun at Magdalena Bay in Baja California is the hottest sun in the world.

Even now when night was close upon us the heat lingered on. The ship and the surrounding bay, the marshes and the mangrove forests, the near islands and the far coasts, all were lost in a leaden haze. Your eyes could not be trusted. What seemed to be one thing turned out to be another. But I was certain of what I saw there below me. It was the drifting form, the arms clasped tight against the body and the face bent downward, of our dead captain, my brother Jeremy.

It is not strange that he was the first I thought of, nor that I felt so certain. Since the night seven days before when he had disappeared from the ship, I had thought of little else. Few liked him, I must confess, for Jeremy Clegg was a hard master. There were some who hated him for his arrogance, and some who envied his good fortune. But to me he had always been a blond-haired, smiling god.

No, not strange that I felt so certain of what I saw floating there in the murky water. Yet as I stood at the rail staring down, what I took to be the body of my brother slowly turned with the tide and nosed against

2

the ship. Peering into the darkness, I now felt that it was much too large to be a human body.

Throughout the day, while we were out searching for the wreck of the *Amy Foster,* a school of hammerheads had followed us and we had shot three of them. But as the object slowly turned again with the changing tide and lay there, half in and half out of the water, I saw that it was not the carcass of one of these marauding sharks.

At this season of the year when the chubascos blow up from the south, they were said to drive before them the trunks of hardwood trees from the jungles of Mexico. The object that gently nudged the side of the ship was of a different size and color from a wind-driven tree.

La Perla reef runs east and west at the entrance to Magdalena Bay. All the month of August and now in September we had searched every spur of it, every cleft and cave, for the sunken hulk of the *Amy Foster.* Islets are scattered near by and the waters around them we had searched also, without success. So the object that I stood staring at had not come from La Perla. Whatever it was, it had floated in from somewhere else, perhaps from the open sea.

I leaned far over the rail. By now the last of the light was gone. All I could make out in the gathered darkness was the outline of something that might be an abandoned boat lying bottom up, one of the canoes that voyaging Indians used on the seas hereabouts. Yet it was too small for a canoe, being not more than seven feet long and half as wide, I judged.

My next thought gave me a start. As the mysterious object had floated into view, at the moment when I decided that it was neither a shark nor the trunk of a tree, I had noted a curious thing about it that I now remembered. Clearly, it had been shaped by human hands, and from wood or else it would not have floated.

I strained my eyes. Was the thing that lay there, hidden by the night, some sort of chest? In past days, so I had been told, Spanish galleons laden with silver and gold had sought refuge here in Magdalena, both from storms and English pirates. If it were a chest — and I began to think that it was — could it have come from one of those treasure ships?

There was something else to support this view. Three days after dropping anchor in Magdalena Bay, we were visited by a band of sea gypsies. They came gliding in at dawn, a dozen or more naked Indians lounging in three canoes. Their chief, who was a wizened little man the color of mud, made signs that he wished to barter. My brother Jeremy motioned him aboard and let down a ladder, but the chief scrambled like a monkey up the anchor chain.

My brother gave him a packet of ship's nails and a length of frayed rope. In return, taking them from his armpits, the chief held out two coins, bit them between his teeth, and dropped them into my brother's hand. They were bright pieces of gold, in shape more round than square, each showing three mountain summits, on one a crowing cock, on another a flame, and on the third a tower.

When asked if he had more coins of this nature, the chief shook his head, slid down the anchor chain, rummaged around in his canoe and scrambled back, holding a piece of a red Spanish shawl. My brother gave him another length of frayed rope, whereupon he motioned for the rest of his followers to climb aboard the ship. This, my brother refused to allow, and the chief left in anger. As the three canoes glided away, the sea gypsies made threatening gestures at us.

Thinking of this encounter, which proved to me that Spanish galleons had been in Magdalena at some time and were probably raided by the Indians, I was more certain than ever that the object that had floated up was a treasure chest.

At this moment, as I stood deep in thought, something brushed against my leg. It was Sapphire, the white bobtailed cat which belonged to my older brother, Caleb. No one in the crew, save myself, and only because I regularly fetched it scraps from the galley, was on good terms with the big cat. In fact, no one took note of him, or at least pretended not to, since he had long claws and an evil disposition. Even a kind word was apt to make him snarl.

I stood back from the rail. Sapphire's presence meant that Caleb Clegg was not far away. A short time later he came hobbling out of his cabin, the heavy boot he wore on his left foot making a shuffling sound on the deck. The bells had rung for supper, so he must have been surprised to find me standing there.

Caleb said nothing, however, but looking up at the night's first star spoke, more, it seemed, to the star than to me.

"In Xanadu did Kubla Khan
    A stately pleasure-dome decree:

7

Where Alph, the sacred river, ran
Through caverns measureless to man
Down to a sunless sea."

He paused and glanced around. Ten years older than I, he towered above me, a tall man and broad of neck and shoulder, but stooped, as if he carried upon his back some heavy burden.

"Aye, 'tis Nathan," he said.

His voice came from far off, deep within him. It was musical to the ear, yet always, since the first time I had heard him speak, it made me uncomfortable. I felt as if his voice did not fit his craggy face and burning gaze, but that someone else, a gentler person, was speaking.

"Dost thou watch the starry islands overhead?" he mused. "Or dost think of lost Jeremy? Or perhaps of thy birthday on the morrow? 'Tis which, the fourteenth, the fifteenth? I do forget."

"The sixteenth," I said.

"Sixteen! The sapling grows. Soon thou will be a man." He tugged at his heavy black beard. "What dost thou wish for a present? Mind thee, it must be simple, since no store lies at hand."

The present I wished for could not be found on the ship or in any store. My wish was to go home, back to Nantucket, as was the wish of everyone aboard the ship, save Caleb Clegg.

"A book," I said, for I liked to read and the bulwarks of his cabin, each nook and cubbyhole, were stacked with books.

"A book it shall be."

He touched me awkwardly on the shoulder and was about to say more when he suddenly withdrew his hand and fell silent. There was, there had been for as long as I could remember, a barrier between us. I suppose it was there because my thoughts and love were centered upon my brother Jeremy. Yet there was another reason, too.

In the silence I heard a faint thump. The sound was twice repeated as the tide pushed at the chest — yes, I was certain now that it was a chest that lay there in the night — and lifted it against the ship's side. I glanced up at my brother, thinking that he too might have heard the sound, but he was lost in thought.

Without another word, he soon clasped his hands behind his back and hobbled off, the big white cat at

his heels. Each evening before supper he made two
rounds of the deck, so I waited until he passed again,
until he opened the door of his cabin and said, casting
a long look at the sky:

> "For he on honey-dew hath fed,
> And drunk the milk of Paradise."

I must say that if my brother Jeremy had been alive
I would not have kept silent about the chest. He would
have been the first I told. But I never thought for a
moment of entrusting my secret to Caleb.

Caleb closed the door behind him. Moving quickly
I made a noose in a long piece of line, threw it over the
side, and after several minutes was able to snare one
end of the floating chest. Taking up the slack, I thrust
the line through a ringbolt and fastened it so as least to
catch the eye of anyone walking along the deck. I then
hurried down the ladderway two steps at a time.

2

Most of our crew were gathered around the mess table eating supper when I came down the ladderway. Except for my friend Tom Waite and Old Man Judd the carpenter, they were the scourings of Nantucket's waterfront. Not many were murderers, I dare say, but there was not one among them who would have balked at the idea. Still, it is difficult to muster men for a long and dangerous voyage, where the rewards hang on the thin thread of chance. To have signed on anyone who was sound of limb for such a wild undertaking was a matter of good fortune.

The men fell silent as I circled the table on my way to the galley. Things would have been different had Jeremy's murderer been found, but whoever it was still walked the decks, ate and slept and worked among us. I say that it would have been different. I am not sure.

A week before the murder the crew were sullen and restless, made so by grievances they imagined and by some that were real.

Our new captain, Troll, who was first mate before my brother's death, sat by himself near the galley door. It was not a place he had chosen or that much pleased him. He wished to have his meals in Jeremy's cabin and had made a row of it when Caleb turned him down.

Mr. Troll had been a harpooneer on one of my father's ships and before that on other Nantucket whalers, a violent role which suited him well. He was a man about thirty, with a thick nose and pale blue eyes. As I passed him, he gave me a nod and a tight-lipped smile.

I scooped up a bowl of the turtle stew our cook made every day, a handful of biscuits, a portion of brown duff pudding, set the tray and took it up the ladder. I didn't enjoy this task of carrying food to the quarterdeck, but since I was the cabin boy my brother Jeremy had ordered me to do it.

"It builds sound character," he said. "Do you want to be a ship's captain someday, like me, or just a second mate on a leaky tub?"

My brother Caleb said nothing. He didn't seem to care one way or the other, so now that Jeremy was dead I kept at the task to show him that I thought Jeremy was right.

I had reached the deck and taken no more than a half-dozen steps when I heard a familiar voice behind me.

"A word," Captain Troll said, sidling up, silent as a shadow. He was fat but quick on his feet. "It's about Mr. Clegg. Of late, since your brother . . . er . . . left us, I've lost his ear. There are things he should know. Perhaps you can pass them along; he'll listen to you."

"Caleb Clegg listens to no one," I said. The force of my words surprised me, yet I was speaking the truth and from my heart. "Least of all to me."

"He must listen to someone," Mr. Troll said, "or else we shall see the decks awash with blood and blood running out the scuppers, yours among it."

"Caleb Clegg goes his own way," I said calmly, though greatly disturbed to hear that Troll thought the crew had reached the point of mutiny. "He has only one purpose and that is to find the wreck of the *Amy Foster*. He's like a . . ."

I fell silent, finding it impossible to speak the harsh word that came to mind, that had been in my mind for many weeks past.

"A madman," Captain Troll answered for me. He spat out the word, like the thrust of a sharp harpoon. "Madman," he said again, lowering his voice. "Why else would he go on day after day on the hunt for a wreck that can never be found. And if it is found, how do we know that the barrels have not been breached and the sperm oil long since leaked away?"

I had recoiled at the word "madman." Hearing it spoken boldly on deck and by Troll had angered me, as did his constant whining.

"Both you and the men took this chance," I said. "Even before we sailed from Nantucket, you knew that in the two years since the *Amy Foster* went down her cargo might have been destroyed. Why do you speak of calamity now?"

Mr. Troll gave a hollow laugh. "Oh, it was a rosy picture he painted then," he said, making a wide gesture with his arms. "A ship crammed from keelson to truck with the finest oil. The hold stacked with oil. Barrels everywhere, even in the galley. A hundred thousand in sperm, mind you, just waiting to be hauled up from Davy's locker, not to mention the barrels of precious ambergris, worth seven dollars an ounce at the nearest apothecary."

15

Anxious to leave Captain Troll, I started off down the deck, but he held out a hand and kept me back.

"A rosy picture, all right," he said, "even to a map of the bay and the sunken reef where the ship was wrecked. There's something suspicious about all of it, if you ask me. Perhaps she wasn't carrying anything at all. Perhaps she was empty . . ."

"You remember the inquiry in Nantucket," I said, "when Caleb Clegg testified about the sinking?"

"I wasn't there."

"But you must have heard about the inquiry; everyone did."

"I heard that Caleb Clegg lost his captain's license, because he was blamed for what happened. I heard that."

"You likewise heard about the ship's cargo," I said. "If you hadn't, then you wouldn't have signed on to find it."

Mr. Troll shuffled his feet. "Well," he muttered, "tell your brother that the crew is in a bad mood. They're tired of hunting for a ghost ship."

I said nothing more and walked along the deck to the door of my brother's cabin. There I waited to see what Troll would do, thinking that he might have

16

heard the chest bumping against the ship's side. But with a quick glance at the sky, he turned and went down the ladderway.

3

I KNOCKED on my brother's door and was told to leave the tray outside. If Caleb was busy at his charts, he never stopped for food. I then went back to the mess room. The men had finished supper and were talking quietly among themselves, but at the sight of me they again grew quiet.

One of my chores was to clean up the table after each meal. Tonight, however, I braved the cook's sharp tongue and walked boldly past him and into the forecastle. My friend, Tom Waite, lay on his bunk, reading a book Caleb had loaned him.

Tom was the diver on our ship, our only diver, until the morning when a mammoth burro clam had fastened on him in ten fathoms of water. After a long struggle he had wrenched himself free from the steel-like jaws, but his left arm had been cruelly cut. For three weeks he hadn't moved from the forecastle and during that time he had taught my brother Caleb the simple rules of his craft. It was necessary if the search for the *Amy Foster* went on that somebody knew how to dive in deep water. Since Caleb among us all was the most determined to find the ship, and therefore perhaps the bravest, the task had fallen upon him.

Tom put down his book. He was four years older than I, quick-tempered, and had a long thin face like a cleaver.

"I've been listening to the talk out there at the supper table," he said. "It appears that most of the crew blame the Indians for the murder, the ones who gave us the gold coins. They think that one or two of them could have crawled up the anchor chain, throttled your brother before he knew what was happening, and then tossed his body into the bay."

"Bert Blanton was not more than fifty feet from the quarterdeck," I said, "and he heard nothing, not a sound. Nobody heard a sound except Old Man Judd. About that time, he says, he heard the cat yowl. Why would the Indians want to kill Jeremy?"

"You remember how the chief got mad when Jeremy wouldn't let him bring the tribe aboard. Well, he might have stayed mad and come back for revenge. They move around quietly and they move fast."

"I still don't know why they would want to kill Jeremy."

Tom ran a hand over his bad arm. "The trouble with you," he said, "is you don't think anyone would want to kill him. You followed Jeremy around as if he was some sort of a god. You couldn't take a deep breath without asking him first. Well, he wasn't that perfect by a long shot. There are a lot of men around who would have liked to kill him. Many a time I felt like killing him myself."

I gave Tom Waite a sharp, questioning glance.

"Jeremy was always so cocksure about everything," he went on, seemingly unperturbed. "Cocksure and if he felt like it, pretty cruel. Take the inquiry in Nantucket. One of the board, Mr. Reynolds, asked him why he hadn't sailed the *Amy Foster* out of the bay when the storm blew up. And what was Jeremy's answer? He drew himself up, straightened his coat — the one with the double row of brass buttons and shining gold anchors on the lapels — lifted his chin and smiled the slow, white-toothed smile that always made the ladies swoon. Then he said in his most cul-

tivated voice, the voice he picked up at college, 'Sir, Captain Caleb Clegg ordered me to stay within the harbor. It was the wrong command, since the bay is shallow and strewn with reefs. Had I been her captain I would have taken the *Amy Foster* out to the open sea where she would have survived the storm. The fact that she was wrecked on La Perla Reef proves me right, Mr. Reynolds.' "

"What's so cocksure, so cruel about that?" I said, angrily.

"It was cocksure to say that the ship wouldn't have been wrecked in the open sea. Ships are wrecked there quite often. And it was cruel to put the blame on Caleb, who was sick at the time, if you remember."

Tom picked up his book, turned the pages, and put it down. "I don't like to bring the matter up," he said, "because . . ."

"It wasn't Caleb who killed Jeremy," I broke in.

Yet, as I spoke, I knew that the murderer could have been my brother. From the morning Caleb and Jeremy had fought in the loft of my father's boat works, over which way a board should be sawn — lengthwise or across — and Caleb had fallen to the ground below, he had hated Jeremy. And that hatred had grown through the years, since, injured in the fall, he was forced to hobble about on a twisted leg, scarred of face, and an object of pity.

"Perhaps it wasn't Caleb after all," Tom said, "but if a man ever had a good reason for murder, it was he."

The crew had left the supper table and I could hear some of them walking around on the deck above. I went out, cleaned up the dishes, washed them and put them away for the morning. Then I hurried back to the forecastle.

"There's some good news after all," I said, sitting down beside Tom on the bunk. "It happened just before supper."

In the glow of the lantern that swung from the beam over our heads, I watched his eyes grow wide as I told him about the chest. "It could be filled with Spanish gold."

"Not filled," Tom said, "or else it wouldn't float. A cubic foot of gold weighs more than a ton, just one cubic foot."

"Perhaps a quarter full."

"Not even that much."

"How much?" I asked, disappointed.

"A bag about the size of your cap," Tom answered.

23

"But the chest could hold something more valuable than that."

"What?"

"A map," Tom said. "A map that shows where a million dollars in gold is hidden away."

Tom laughed, we both laughed because we had begun to sound like a couple of adventurous schoolboys.

"What shall I do with the chest?" I said. "It will have to be moved before daylight."

"Tow it ashore," Tom said. "Find a good place in the cove and hide it."

We talked for a while about the map, counting the gold we would find after following all the instructions. When the men started to drift down from above we still went on counting the gold and how we would spend it. But we pretended that we were spending our share of the sperm oil and ambergris in the sunken hold of the *Amy Foster*.

"You'll both have barnacles on your beards before she's found," said Jim Still.

"Shut up," the cook said. "And you, Nathan, see to it that the dishes are cleaned up when they ought to be."

I waited until everyone was asleep, or seemed to be, before I went quietly up the ladder to carry out the plan Tom and I had decided upon.

4

A HALF-MOON had climbed the sky and everything around me shone clearly — the ship, the flat waters of the bay, and the beach on Isla Madera. A dark night would have been better for what I had to do, but I did not dare to wait for the moon to set.

Blanton, who had the midnight watch, was out of sight at the stern of the ship. I found that the tide had caught up the chest and that it was pointed toward the open sea, straining hard at its tether. I untied the line from the ringbolt and dropped it overboard.

Alert, our small barquentine, carried four launches. Three of them were in the water, tied to the anchor chain, all of them stacked with diving gear and heavy to handle. But there was no choice, for while the fourth launch swung empty in its davits, I could not lower it away without help.

I ran to the bow and slid down the chain and scrambled into the nearest launch. Setting the oars in the locks, I headed out in the direction I thought the chest would drift, now that it had been set free, and by good fortune overtook it after a time of hard rowing. With the chest in tow, I turned and made a wide circle around the ship and set a course for Isla Madera, which was some mile or more to the north.

Alert lay to starboard, its trim, black hull clearly outlined by the moon. Two men stood at the stern and

I supposed that they were watching me. It did not matter, for from the distance that separated us, they could not tell that I had something in tow. Nor would my absence cause any alarm. The past week I had taken to rowing at night, just to be away from the ship.

The tide was against me, running toward the channel and the shore. An hour passed before I reached a narrow point fringed with low-lying mangroves and above them a white, hat-shaped peak where shorebirds nested. Rounding this point, I came to a sandy cove and here I beached the launch. By daylight the cove was within view of the ship, so I untied the chest and waded through the shallows and pushed it up the beach to where the mangroves grew.

I could see that the chest was heavily encrusted with barnacles and trailing weeds, as if it had long been in the water. Yet, as I had noted before, it was not formless. About three feet in depth and a full seven feet in length, it was somewhat smaller at one end than the other. At one moment it seemed to be a small canoe. Then, as the moonlight struck in a different way, it looked like a big Nantucket coffin, the kind that my grandfather was buried in.

With great effort I pushed the chest back into the

mangroves, tied the line taut to a mangrove root and broke off some branches and carefully covered it over, for fear that it would be seen by daylight. Our men gathered clams in the cove and twice I had noticed Indian canoes pulled up on the beach. I then rowed back to the ship, planning to come back at my first chance with the tools, a hammer and bar, to pry the chest open.

Instead of finding Blanton on deck, as I expected, it was Captain Troll who greeted me.

"A fine night for rowing," he said.

"Yes," I said. But a pool of water already was forming where I stood and my clothes were smeared with mud. There was no use to pretend that I had been out for a row. "I went to the cove to catch a mess of clams," I said, trying to make a joke of it.

Captain Troll laughed. "The way you look, the clams caught *you*."

Troll was curious, but I was sure that he had not seen the chest. I said good-night and walked on toward the ladderway.

"Did you speak a word to your brother?" he called after me.

I turned around. "No," I said. I should have addressed him as "sir," but this I found hard to do and for some reason he did not demand it. "He was locked in his cabin."

"And for two days hasn't dived," Troll said, walking to where I stood. "Let's leave your brother out of it. Just the two of us can talk."

In the moonlight his thin, straight mouth seemed changed, even friendly.

"After all," he said, "you're part owner of this ship."

"Not until I reach the age of twenty-one."

"That's looking at things in a legal way, not a sensible way," Troll said. "For weeks you've noticed how the men scamp their work, how they shirk on deck, grumble at this and that. Since your brother Jeremy . . . well, left us, they're worse. Suspicious of each other, wondering all the time who's going to be killed next. They didn't like Jeremy much, but he made them toe the line. Caleb, they don't like at all, and what he says they laugh at."

"You are captain of the *Alert*," I said. "It's your duty to see that they don't laugh."

"Remember," Troll said, "there's only two of us who care what happens to the ship, you and me. The rest we can't count on, even Caleb Clegg, him the least

of all. And against us are a dozen men who would as
leave toss us in the bay as not."

"There's nothing I can do about it. I am only the
cabin boy. They'd laugh at me, too, if I gave them
orders."

Troll walked down the deck and came back and
cleared his throat. "You're wrong. There's something

you can do," he said. "As part owner of the ship, give me the order to raise anchor and in two hours we'll be at sea, homeward bound."

"If I gave this order, then you wouldn't be to blame. Is that what you mean?"

"Exactly. If I take matters into my own hands, against Caleb Clegg, I would be tried for mutiny the day we reach Nantucket."

"I'll talk to my brother in the morning," I said, starting toward the ladderway.

Troll grasped my arm. The waning moon no longer softened the face that now was thrust toward me.

"Talk is useless," he said. "Give the order and I'll put Caleb Clegg in irons, where he should be."

The order was on my tongue to say. Yet standing there on the deck of a ship that one day would be part mine by rightful inheritance, knowing full well that at any moment she might be seized by a mutinous crew, that Caleb's life and Tom Waite's life and my own were in danger, and that the chances of ever finding the sunken ship were small, still I did not give the order.

It was not my fear of the Caleb Clegg whom Troll knew that held me back. Or the Caleb Clegg who would see the ship rot beneath his feet rather than forsake his mad search for the *Amy Foster*. No, it was not this man, but another. It was my *brother* Caleb Clegg I feared, whom I had feared since first I could remember and through all the years of my childhood. I suppose it was his scarred face, his hobbling walk, his curious way of speaking that repelled me and was the reason for my fear. I could have feared him because he hated Jeremy, or because he chose his own grim path and asked nothing of anyone. I don't know.

I glanced astern, down the deserted deck where a light shone through the open door of my brother's cabin. I saw him standing at his table, with the chart of Magdalena Bay spread out before him. He stood with his massive head thrown back, black hair, raven black once but now streaked with gray, falling around his face, hands clenched at his sides.

Then I saw that his eyes were not on the chart, as first I had thought, but upon people who were not there. He faced them defiantly. It was the same look I had seen as he stood before the court on that bright April morning in Nantucket, now more than a year ago. He had stood in just this way, with his hands clenched and his head thrown back, listening silently while Purcell, the first mate, and his brother Jeremy had testified against him. He did not move when he heard himself blamed for the sinking of the *Amy Foster,* or when he heard the fateful words that stripped him of his captain's license. Nor did he move until everyone had gone but me. Only then did he hobble out into the sunshine, his head still erect.

"Give the order to sail," Troll said.

For a moment more I watched my brother. I watched until he leaned over the table and began to study the chart of Magdalena Bay. Without answering Captain Troll, I bade him good-night and went below.

In my bunk I lay awake, trying to think of what I would say to Caleb when I talked to him about our restless crew. I was determined to do so, although I feared there was nothing I could say that would change the course he steadfastly pursued or hasten the hour of our return to Nantucket.

I was certain that my brother Jeremy had come to Magdalena Bay for only one reason — to salvage the rich harvest of sperm oil and ambergris which lay in the hold of the wrecked *Amy Foster* — for he had talked of little else until the day of his death. But my brother Caleb never spoke of it, to me nor to anyone. There was something far different he was searching for. Had it something to do with the inquiry in Nantucket? Could it be the logbook of the *Amy Foster*? I wondered. If it were, then the search would go until the crew mutinied or the ship was found.

The sky was turning gray before I slept and when I awoke it was to sounds outside. I took them to be the chest bumping against the ship, until I remembered that the chest lay hidden a mile away in the mangroves on Isla Madera.

5

THAT MORNING Captain Troll ordered us all on deck and to the mainmast.

The day dawned clear but already a blanket of heat had settled over the ship. The men stood around in sullen groups of two or three, waiting to hear why they had been called, hopeful that it would be word that the *Alert* was sailing home at last. Captain Troll also waited. From time to time he gave me a questioning glance as if I might know why we were there. I knew no more than he did, except that we were not sailing back to Nantucket.

Caleb came limping along the deck. In one hand he carried a wooden maul and in the other two bright coins, the golden doubloons we had received from the Indian chief. He burnished the coins on his sleeve and with two square nails he nailed them to the mast. Stepping back, he then surveyed the men who had gathered around him. He looked from one to the other in turn, calling them by name.

"Whoever among you," he said, "doth find the wreck of the *Amy Foster,* it is he who shall have yon Spanish coins. Sharpen thine eyes and hone thine wits, therefore. Each golden piece is worth a full year's pay."

The faces of the crew brightened somewhat at this news. Still, for men who had dreamed of riches, of a shipload of sperm oil and ambergris, it meant little.

"Whilst pondering in the night," Caleb went on, "there hath come to mind a likely spot, past which strange currents writhe and run and where the *Amy Foster* hath drifted. There we shall find our ship and when 'tis done my share of oil and ambergris I shall divide among thee equally."

Since this was better news by far than the offer of two Spanish coins to one lucky man, the crew went off in high spirits. The launches were manned and rowed down the bay to the new place Caleb had chosen. It was about a mile from the ship and closer to the mangroves, so close, indeed, that I could make

out the path I had left and the mound of branches where the chest lay hidden.

We moored the launches in a wide circle, around the chosen spot, and set up the diving platform. The platform held a two-handed pump, which forced the air into the hose that fed the diver. Hitherto, we all had taken turns at the pump, but on this morning my brother gave the task to old Judd and me. It was a clear sign that he no longer trusted any of the crew save us. The others were sent off to dive on their own, using goggles made of wood and glass.

Judd and I got my brother into his suit, which did not fit him so well as it did Tom Waite, and began to push up and down on the handle. Caleb slipped over the side and disappeared in a cloud of bubbles. He was clumsy and could not go down in the deep waters, but through determination he still had become a diver.

Judd was a grizzled old man of forty or more, with cold blue eyes and a bad temper. I had not liked him much when first we had left Nantucket, but during the time at sea and the weeks at Magdalena he had proven to be a friend. While I pushed at the heavy handle, I cast a glance toward the mangroves. The mound of branches stood up so clear by daylight that I was sure that sooner or later someone would see it. Tom Waite would not be able to go there with me for at least another week, so I told the old man about the chest. He would know best how to open it, since he was the ship's carpenter.

The old man listened to me silently, as if a chest of Spanish gold was of no interest. But I noticed that the pump handle soon began to move up and down at a faster rate, and from time to time he would pause to give the mangroves a sidelong look.

"We'll go over tonight," he said at last. "I'll take along a chisel and hammer and we'll open her up. Why would a Spaniard, though I've known some crazy ones in my life, hide gold in a chest seven feet long? Chances are she's empty."

"My grandfather had a Spanish chest which was six feet long," I said, speaking half the truth.

At noon my brother signaled that he wanted to come to the surface and we pulled him in. By then a hot land wind had risen and white-capped waves were racing across the bay. Besides, the hammerheads had begun to swim around the launch, so Caleb decided to quit diving for that day.

Judd and I seized our chance and took the small boat, saying that we were going to hunt for abalones, and rowed off to the cove. As we ran the boat up the beach, I saw two of the other men following us. It turned out that they had come for abalones, too, so we had to lose ourselves among the rocks until they left. When they were out of sight, we took off our shoes and waded into the mangroves.

A pair of black, long-beaked hell-divers sat preening themselves on the mound of branches that covered the chest. As we came upon them, they rose with wild, chilling cries and flew away. To me they were ill omens, but the old man said that the hell-diver was a sure sign of good fortune, that two hell-divers were twice as good.

He had brought along a rusty hatchet, which I wanted him to use on the chest, but the old man was against it.

"It's the chest we got to think about," he said. "Might have belonged to an Egyptian king. The thing's full of air, most likely."

The barnacles grew in dense clusters, one cluster upon another, small ones upon big ones the size of a gull's egg. Thus, the six sides of the massive chest were encased in an armor of shell, the whole of a faint, pinkish color.

"It's been in the sea a long time," the old man said, "before you were born, maybe."

Setting to work with the hatchet, Judd chipped away at the top of the chest, which was some five inches above the water. He worked slowly, with his tongue between his teeth, studying each stroke before he made it, as if he were working on a jewel.

"At this rate," I said, "we'll never know what's in the chest."

The old man did not reply but went on, thoughtfully chipping away at the chest. He even stopped to light a pipe and stand for a time examining a space no larger than his hand which it had taken him more than an hour to clean off.

"Smooth as silk," he said, running a finger over the wood he had laboriously bared to the sun. "Planed and rubbed by a master of the trade, whoever he was."

Watching him, realizing that he was far more interested in the chest itself than in what was hidden inside, I made up my mind that as soon as Tom Waite was well, together we would open the chest in a hurry.

The old man chipped away until night came and then we carefully put the branches back on top of the chest and waded out of the mangroves, taking care not to leave any signs.

6

At suppertime I carried a tray of food to my brother's cabin. He was standing in front of the table again. Before him lay the chart of Magdalena, which he had made and was always changing. The tides and currents as he knew them were marked in green, waving lines and the places where we had searched for the lost ship, with red circles.

"What thinkest thou of this watery stretch," he said, motioning me to the table and placing a finger upon the chart, "southward here from Rehusa Strait and close by yon small isle? Dost look promising to thee?"

He often asked me questions like this, not expecting an answer and more to put his mind in order, I believe, than for any other reason. For the first time, I decided to say what I thought.

Since we had dived that morning within plain sight

of the mangroves, it was wiser for me to agree with him that the new spot seemed promising. Where we searched, it mattered little, for I strongly doubted that we would ever find the *Amy Foster*. Yet the slump of his shoulders and the white cast of his face touched me for a moment.

"You thought this morning that you had found the right place," I said. "We haven't finished diving there. There's nothing to gain by hopping around all over the bay like a chicken. Let's go back and search again."

Surprised, Caleb glanced up. Then he walked past me to the door and for a long time looked out into the night.

"Thunder and lightning that day," he said at last in his far-off voice, "a southeast wind blowing, stronger far than any wind that blows around the Horn. A foul and fearsome day, Nathan, the spinning world aswirl about our battered ears, our eyes cringing in their sockets. Yet well I remember where the ship went down."

He walked back to the table and put his finger hard upon the chart. " 'Twas here. Aye, here upon La Perla Reef."

"When the ship went down," I said, "you were in the cabin, out of your head with fever."

"Aye, but whilst carried ashore by the raging tide, in that brief moment before my senses did depart, I didst glimpse the rocks which mark the reef."

He again placed a finger upon the outlines of La Perla Reef. " 'Twas here, I tell thee, here. But wherever, here or there or yonder, 'twas a needless thing. Plainly I wrote in the log, which now lies lost somewhere about us. I wrote it for thy brother Jeremy, knowing that the fever hadst stealthily crept upon me. 'Beware the southern storm,' I wrote. 'Do not be caught in Magdalena. Take the ship to sea. Heed my command, Jeremy, take the . . .' "

Suddenly Caleb stopped. He stepped back from the chart table and passed a hand across his eyes. For a while he did not move, but stood staring straight before him.

"You had a chance to testify," I said, "to tell Captain Wills and Captain Sterne and Mr. Reynolds what you have just told me. Yet you heard the testimony against you and spoke not a word to defend yourself. Why?"

Caleb turned his eyes slowly toward me. They had

a lost and wandering look. He said, "Why? Why? 'Tis possible, Nathan, that I didst write nothing in the log. 'Tis possible that I did dream it all."

Once more he passed a hand across his eyes. Then, limping to the doorway, he looked up at the evening sky. I think that he was already sorry for what he had said. It is likely that he had meant to relive that moment before the storm only for himself and not for me.

I was about to leave when he turned around and smiled, a rare thing for him.

"Hath slipped my mind about thy birthday," he said. " 'Tis thy sixteenth among us. Come, I have a gift for thee."

I never entered my brother's cabin without the thought that it was an old bookshop on some dusty byway of London, which Charles Dickens might have written about. Books were scattered everywhere. Stacked against the bulwarks, they framed the two portholes. They lay on the bunk and underfoot. To reach the small table where Caleb ate his meals, you had to take a crooked path and each step carefully, as if you were traveling through a thicket. And the cabin had about it the musty smell of an old bookshop, with nothing of the sea.

Caleb swung his arms up and made a fulsome gesture. "A book, I wish to give thee," he said. "Search and find one that suits thy temper."

Looking about here and there, on the bunk and under it and along the bulwarks, I at last saw a book that struck my fancy. It was called *Moby-Dick: or, The Whale,* a large tome bound in green and gold leather, written by an author named Herman Melville.

"I like stories about whales and whaling," I said, tucking the book under my arm. "I guess it's natural that I do, since I've heard of little else from the time I was in the cradle."

My brother gave me a curious glance. A frown crossed his forehead and I had the feeling that I had taken a book which he especially prized. I was about to put it back and select another, when he stopped me.

" 'Tis odd that thou like this one," he said, "but take it with thee. 'Tis a true leviathan of a book and thou shalt learn from it much of the whale and his ways, enough to beguile the hours of thy youth. When older thou may find among its dire circumambulations

47

things to give thee pause. And if thou art deserving, knowledge of an uncommon kind. Aye, a true leviathan. Perhaps thou art right to hold it gingerly as thou do, between thumb and forefinger. Who knows? Who knows?"

Caleb threaded his way to the table and once again began to study the chart of Magdalena. Then, of a sudden, he glanced up as if he had just remembered that I was still in the cabin.

"I would not give thee the book," he said, "unless I knew it all by heart. Aye, every word from truck to keelson, fore and aft and amidships. Now avast and leave me to muse upon the problem alone. I venture that thou shalt find Captain Ahab better company."

Again I tucked *Moby-Dick: or, The Whale* under my arm and walked through the litter of books toward the door. Caleb's birthday present was the first gift I had ever received from him. As I reached for the door catch, the thought crossed my mind to tell him about the chest I had found. At that moment the heavy book slipped and fell with a clatter of fluttering pages.

Caleb glanced up. "Take care," he said in one of his softest voices. " 'Tis not a ball to kick about."

I stiffly thanked him for his gift and went below and sat down to supper with the book propped in front of me. The crew had gone above for air, so the forecastle was quiet. I found the first pages of much interest, being in the form of short writings about whales and whaling, collected from over the world. There were writings from the time of King Alfred, even from the Bible, and such things as "The aorta of a whale is larger than the main pipe of the waterworks at London Bridge."

Later that night I fixed a fat candle to the bulkhead and lay in my bunk and began the story of *Moby-Dick: or, The Whale*. First I read the chapter names. There were one hundred and thirty-five of them, a goodly number, besides an Epilogue, which in a way is a chapter too. All of them sounded exciting, especially such names as "The Pequod Meets the Rose Bud," "The Doubloon," "Fast Fish and Loose Fish," and "Ambergris."

There was also a chapter called "Ahab." As I read the word I recalled that when I had taken leave of my brother he had said, "Thou shalt find Captain Ahab better company." I therefore turned to this chapter and began to read. Not far along, I came upon a

description of Ahab: "Threading its way out from among his grey hairs, and continuing right down one side of his tawny scorched face and neck, till it disappeared in his clothing, you saw a slender rod-like mark, lividly whitish."

These words amazed me. They could have been written, every one of them, to describe the scar that disfigured my brother's face.

Farther on I happened on this: ". . . not a little of this overbearing grimness was owing to the barbaric white leg upon which he partly stood. It had previously come to me that this ivory leg had at sea been fashioned from the polished bone of the sperm whale's jaw. 'Aye, he was dismasted off Japan,' said the old Gay-Head Indian once; 'but like his dismasted craft, he shipped another mast without coming home for it. He has a quiver of 'em.' "

This also amazed me. For though my brother did not have an ivory leg, let alone a quiver of them, he did stand upon a leg that was stiff at the knee and short by a full two inches.

I quit at this point and somewhat unsettled went to sleep pondering what I had read.

7

Soon after dawn we went back to the place where we had searched the previous day, anchored the launches in a circle, and set up the pump. As my brother was getting ready to go down for his first dive, two trim canoes filled with Indians came from the direction of Rehusa Strait. Each canoe carried six paddles and they pulled up beside our big launch and waved a friendly greeting.

The little, mud-colored chief we had met before held out a handful of pearls. Caleb let him know that we wished to barter, and by making the sign of a ship, one that lay beneath the water, and the motions of diving, he was able to strike a bargain.

As a result of the signs, repeated over and over for the better part of an hour, and the gift of an iron bar the chief sent out his men to look for the *Amy Foster*.

These Indians were fine divers. They regularly dived for abalones and scallops, which they ate, and for pearls which, they told us, they took eastward on foot across the high mountains to barter for cloth.

It was a good bargain. With eight of our men diving and twelve of theirs (the little chieftain did not dive, but sat in his canoe, eyeing the pump) we covered a wide circle that day. At sunset, after Caleb had given him a piece of leaky hose and three broken screws, the chief promised to bring his men back the next morning. They left us, skimming the water like flying fish, and disappeared around a headland that lay to the north.

That night Judd and I set off with a lantern and fishlines. We said that we were going out to catch sierra, but hidden in our clothes were the proper tools to use on the chest. We fished our way toward the cove. When we reached the cove we doused the lantern and waded into the mangroves. Then we uncovered the chest, and Judd set to with chisel and hammer.

He worked as he had before, like a jeweler cutting gems, yet the work went faster and by the time we were ready to leave, he had cleaned off an area about four feet square. It seemed to form an end, the larger end of the chest, where one of the sides joined the top.

"Shine the lantern close," he said, and when I did he tested the wood with a thumbnail. "A strange kind of wood," he said. "I've never seen its likes before. Tough as iron. Good wood, good carpenter, I'd say."

We covered the chest as we had before and hid the tools. On our way back to the ship Judd lighted the lantern and put out two lines and started to fish for sierra.

"Something to show Captain Troll," the old man said. "He's got his eye on us, me especially. Ever since the murder, he's been snooping around, acting like a policeman."

The old man jerked on his line, waited and jerked again and pulled in a silver-sided fish as long as his arm. He unhooked the fish, straightened the feathers on the jig, and threw it over the side while I rowed on toward the ship.

Then he said, "Appears to me that your brother should hold court and talk to everyone, call them in one by one and find out what they know."

"Caleb's not going to do that," I said. "He told

me the night after the murder that the best idea was
to wait until the ship docked in Nantucket and turn
everything over to the regular court."

"For instance," the old man said, "there're a few
things I haven't told."

55

"You heard the big white cat yowl about an hour before dawn."

"Yes, and an infernal racket it was, too."

Judd had another fish on the line and I quit rowing until he brought it in.

"What else do you know?" I said.

"Well, I heard a voice about that time. Talking to the cat, I guess."

"Whose voice?" I asked.

"I couldn't be sure, but it sounded like Caleb's. Then I heard a cabin door slam shut. But a short while later, perhaps a minute, I heard someone walking along the deck, going toward the forecastle. I know Caleb's walk, sort of a thump, but it wasn't his. It sounded more like the way Troll walks. Kind of jerky and fast, as though whoever it was might be in a hurry."

The old man tossed the jig overboard and I began to row toward the ship. Around us the waters were black, but we left a long trail of phosphorescence and fiery drops fell from my oars. Whenever I turned to glance at the ship, her decks seemed deserted except for a man standing watch at the stern.

Yet once again, Captain Troll met us as we crawled

over the rail. He glanced at the two fish and the lantern and for a long time at the hatchet which I held in my hand, it being too large to hide.

"You have a new way to catch fish," he said.

"Yes," the old man answered. "Nathan here shines the light around and when the fish come up to find out what's happening, I just hit them over the head with the hatchet."

Troll gave one of his small coughs. He might even have smiled in his tight-lipped way, I could not tell. But as we walked on along the deck and went down the ladderway, Judd said that we had better wait and not go to the cove the next day, and I agreed.

But on the second day, when we planned to go back to the island, one of the Indians, who was the best of the divers and could stay underwater for a full three minutes, discovered the wreck of the *Amy Foster*.

8

The ship lay in ten fathoms of water, about a mile from the cove and the mangroves, wedged at the foot of a shallow reef. Looking down through the clear currents that swirled around her, you could see her wavering form, the masts broken off at the deck, and dim, trailing pieces of canvas that once were sails.

There was jubilation among the crew when the Indians brought news of the discovery. The little chief, whose name was Bonsig, came flying over the water with his three canoes and pulled in at the launch as my brother was resting between dives. The chief pointed northward toward Isla Ballena, then downward several times, drawing in the air the outlines of a ship.

We raised our anchors and made ready to follow him, but first he demanded gifts. Fascinated by the wheezing noise, his choice was the pump. At last he settled for a hammer, a pocket comb which one of the men owned, six square nails, all of them bent, and two torn cotton shirts, one belonging to Blanton and the other to me.

We left the cove and followed Chief Bonsig up the bay and past a small island. He kept pointing ahead, but we could see that he had not left a float to mark the site of the wreck, and for a while we feared that he would not find it again. Yet, like a homing bird, he went straight to the place, and now clothed in my torn shirt, stood up in the canoe and gave us a toothless grin, then a speech in a language which I took to be Spanish.

We anchored the boats midst wild shouts and singing. The men had forgotten their grievances, or at least had laid them aside — how only a few days before they had watched my brother dive and quietly wondered how they could cut his air hose without being caught. They even gave three loud cheers for the *Alert,* the finest ship that ever sailed out of Nantucket, and three for Caleb Clegg. My brother must have heard the cheers as we bolted on his helmet, but he gave no sign.

The bay was calm except for a pod of whales that swam about in the distance and sent up misty fountains and struck the water thunderous blows with their mighty flukes. Everyone, including the Indians, pulled in and anchored around the diving launch. There were many offers of help, but Judd and I refused them and set the pump in motion.

The crew cheered again when Caleb slipped over the side and went down in a whirling cloud of bubbles. I saw him reach the deck of the ship and walk slowly along it, a small school of fish swimming beside him. Then, as he drew near the forward hold and bent over to examine the hatch, the movement of the hose disturbed the silt that had gathered upon the wreck and he was lost to view.

My brother was not down long, for it was near nightfall, and he brought back little news, but the men cheered him again. We rowed off to the ship and took the pump with us, fearing that the Indians would steal it in the night.

There were more songs at supper and much laughter. It was a different ship from the one I had been living aboard. But I knew how suddenly their mood would change if Caleb found that the cargo of the

Amy Foster had drifted away through some hole rent in her bottom.

After supper I took Caleb his tray of food. He was standing at the door of his cabin, with his gaze fixed upon the horizon. He did not speak and I put the tray where the big cat could not reach it. I was leaving when he called out to me.

"Avast there," he said. "How dost thou fare with the Whale? Dost the white monster excite thee? And what of Captain Ahab who pursueth it over the world's far seas? Yes, what of Ahab? How doth he strike thee?"

"I've not read all the book," I said.

"How far hast thee trod?"

"As far as chapter fifty-eight."

"Thou readest fast."

"I skip parts."

Caleb laughed. "Thou skip because thou fiercely pursuest something and do not wish to be checked by wily circumlocutions. Chapter fifty-eight? Oh, yes, I recall it. It goes, 'Consider the sea; how its most dreaded creatures glide under water, unapparent for the most part, and treacherously hidden beneath the loveliest tints of azure . . . Consider, once more,

the universal cannibalism of the sea; all whose creatures prey upon each other . . . Consider all this;
and then turn to this green, gentle, and most docile
earth; consider them both, the sea and the land;
and do you not find a strange analogy to something
in yourself? For as this appalling ocean surrounds the
verdant land, so in the soul of men there lies one in-
sular Tahiti, full of peace and joy, but encompassed by
all the horrors of the half known life. God keep thee!
Push not off from the isle, thou canst never return!' "

Caleb paused, took from his mouth the pipe he was
smoking, and threw it, still lighted, into the waters
beneath.

" 'What business have I with this pipe?' " he said.

" 'This thing that is meant for sereneness, to send up
mild vapors among white hairs . . . I'll smoke no
more . . .' not until the log is found. But tell me,
Nathan, what dost thou think of Ahab? In thy reading of the book, surely thou hast come upon him ere
now?"

I recalled, as Caleb paused to throw his lighted pipe
away and explain why he had done so, that I had read
in *Moby-Dick* a description of this same curious act.
Captain Ahab himself had thrown his lighted pipe

away, giving up his right to peace while the White Whale still lived in the sea.

Some of the things that long had puzzled me about Caleb became clearer in my mind. I saw that his own misfortunes at some time in the past had drawn him toward the luckless Ahab. Both men had riven faces, both walked with difficulty, my brother upon a short and twisted leg, Ahab upon one of ivory. Moreover, Ahab had vowed to search out and slay the White Whale that had maimed him; my brother had sworn to find the *Amy Foster,* whose loss had likewise maimed him.

"What dost think of Captain Ahab," my brother asked again, "so far in thy readings of him?"

Yet at this moment, with Caleb's gaze fixed upon me, I doubted that he was aware that his appearance, his acts, his words were those of Captain Ahab. There was a secret sympathy between them, that was all. He was not slavishly acting out a part, a role which he had devised. He was not Captain Ahab, but a man tortured in body and mind who had read of Ahab and in time unknowingly had become Ahab.

"From what I've seen of him," I said, "he's to be pitied."

"He would not welcome thy pity," Caleb answered.

"I suppose not," I said. I wanted to say, "Both of you are madmen, and madmen have no need of pity."

"Dost think Ahab right? Would thou pursuest a fiend that hath snatched a limb from off thy body?"

"No. I'd be afraid that he might snatch another limb. Perhaps my life, too."

"Thou would rather live half a man and see thy enemy go unscathed? But I shalt not ask thee more until thou finish with the book and knowest Ahab's inner workings. Avast, get thee at it."

I left him there in the doorway looking off across the moonlit waters, climbed into my bunk, and opened the book where I had stopped reading. As I read on, whenever Captain Ahab came into the story, it was not he whom I saw standing alone upon the quarter-deck or shouting commands into the wind, but my brother, Caleb Clegg.

9

AT GRAY dawn we sailed north toward Isla Ballena, closer to the sunken ship. With the sun we were ready to dive. Again, each man of the crew was eager to work at the pump. Even the little Indian chief wanted to take a hand, though the air was hard to breathe and the sun was fierce. My brother grimly smiled at all the eagerness and while Judd bolted on his suit, from within the brass-bound helmet I heard something that sounded like a hollow laugh.

Our four launches were anchored in a circle around the wreck. The men crawled to the gunwales and cheered once more as Caleb went down. The water was clear except for myriads of small fish that had found a home in the sunken ship. I saw him reach the deck, brushing the fish away from his helmet as if they were so many flies, and disappear into the hold.

When half an hour passed without a signal of any
kind, uneasiness began to spread from boat to boat.
Blanton wondered how he could find the barrels of
ambergris among all the hundreds of barrels that held
sperm oil. Second mate Still doubted that one man

could handle the heavy barrels by himself. Everyone had a question or some uneasy doubt.

The men fell silent as another half hour went by, then a faint signal came along the line, four short pulls twice repeated, telling us to send down the grappling hook and chain. We watched the gear go down, Caleb crawl out and drag it back into the hold. Minutes passed, the ship's bells struck nine, struck the half hour, then the signal came to haul.

It took the strength of three men, heaving hand over hand, to bring the line in. Nearly the size of a hogshead, the cask came up in slow circles, like a hooked shark that had grown tired. Trailing weeds covered most of it, but as it drew close to the surface I clearly saw, burned deep in the rounded top, the letter A.

" 'A' stands for ambergris," Troll said.

"Two hundred pounds of ambergris," said Blanton who had helped to haul it in, "or more."

"Two hundred pounds worth seven dollars an ounce," someone said in a shaky voice.

The cask was hauled into the launch and an ax found to breach it. Captain Troll hesitated, thinking no doubt that Caleb Clegg should be there to oversee such an important undertaking. But the angry mutterings of the crew quickly changed his mind, and with one blow he split the oaken top.

Slowly, as we pressed around the barrel, there oozed from it a small gobbet of dull-gray matter, waxy soft. We all, except Captain Troll, stared down at the unpleasant sight. I had never seen ambergris before, but surely this was not the fabled substance from which perfume was made, such things as pastiles and hair powder and precious candles, and which the Turks carried reverently in their caravans to Mecca.

Captain Troll thrust a finger into the gray gobbet and waved it under our noses. I was suddenly enveloped in fragrance, so powerful, so enchanting that it made my senses reel.

The only one who was not awed by the ambergris was Chief Bonsig. He reached up and pushed his nose into it, then backed away, made a horrible face, and climbed back into his canoe, where he sat as though numbed.

"The barrel's worth twenty thousand dollars," said Captain Troll.

"And there's more to come," Blanton said.

"If what Caleb Clegg said is true," Troll added.

Again we let down the grappling hook. Silent and

breathless, the men watched while Caleb picked up the hook and carried it into the hold. An hour went by, but I knew that my brother was not looking for ambergris.

At last he signaled and we pulled him in, taking a long time to do so lest he suffer from quick-changing pressures. As the brass-bound helmet was lifted off his shoulders, I saw that his face was white and drawn from the hours below. Yet the grim smile that I had seen when he went down still was there.

"When do you dive again?" Blanton asked.

"How many barrels did you see?" Captain Troll asked.

A chorus of questions followed, but my brother did not answer them. He stood looking around at the peaceful waters of the bay, at the whales playing, at the ship, and the hot sky. At last he looked at the row of grinning faces.

"Dost thou now believe Caleb Clegg?" he said hoarsely. "Sailors of fair weather and shirkers of the storm, tell me, art thou now of a different mind than oft before?"

"Aye!" spoke the crew as one, each man at that

moment willing to suffer whatever insult that might be heaped upon him.

"Dost thou now wish to remain at Magdalena until yon rich harvest is gathered in?"

"Aye," came the answer, every man knowing that without Caleb Clegg more casks of ambergris might never be found. "Aye, aye!"

Without further words Caleb turned his back upon them and had me row him to the ship. Nor did he confide in me, as he sat in the stern staring out over the bay. Yet I was aware that he had sent up the barrel of ambergris and promised the men still a richer harvest, only to buy the time he would need to find the log of the *Amy Foster*. And find it he would, no matter how long it might take him.

10

Aᴏᴛᴇʀ ᴡᴇ had eaten supper, the old man and I went quietly off to the cove. There was no need to make excuses for our leaving. Indeed, no one saw us go. The barrel had been rolled into the forecastle, and when we left, the men were sitting around it, merrily drinking the jug of rum my brother had sent along, sniffing the heady fragrance that not only had the power to make a man feel drunk, but also was worth seven dollars an ounce.

The sky was clear except for a line of puffy clouds low in the south. Since the moon was nearly full, work on the chest went faster than before. In two hours Judd had chipped away the last of the barnacles.

With hatchet and claw hammer, we then set about the lid. It was held tight, water-tight, by oakum and pitch, as well as by square nails set two inches apart and deeply driven into the unyielding wood. It would have been far easier just to bash in the lid, but again the old man refused.

Prying at the smaller end of the chest, which was square and of a different shape from the larger end, we managed to unloosen four of the corner nails and draw them out. All the while the old man cautioned me to take care not to injure the wood.

It was past eleven o'clock by now, so we hid the tools and covered the chest with branches, as usual, and made our way back toward the cove. We had reached the edge of the mangroves, when at the same moment we saw beyond us a boat lying beside ours on the beach. The old man grasped my arm and instantly we drew back into the shadowed brush. A voice hailed us not more than a dozen paces away. It was Captain Troll and he was sauntering toward us, puffing on his pipe.

"At the clams again?"

Neither Judd nor I answered.

"I didn't know that you found them on trees," he said.

"Not *on* trees," Judd said, "but all around them."

Troll looked at us as we stood there empty-handed.

"Where are they? The two of you have been out here since suppertime. You should have a bushel by now."

I thought it wiser to tell him about the chest, but kept my silence and hoped that the old man would think of something to say.

"We've been hunting ducks," Judd said. "They nest out here at night."

"Yes, I've seen them flying," Troll said. "But you had poor luck. You'd have better luck if you took a gun."

"Yes," the old man said, weakly.

We walked down the beach, Troll falling into step behind us. As we slid our boat into the water, Troll took hold of the old man's arm and jerked him around.

"What are you up to?" Troll said. "The two of you have been coming here every night. You don't think I believe it's to catch clams and hunt ducks, do you?"

The old man pulled his arm from Troll's grasp. "Believe what you want," he said.

"What I want, is it?" said Troll. "Well, I believe that you've found something that's drifted here from the wreck, something valuable."

The old man said nothing and I picked up the oars and set them in the locks and began to row.

Captain Troll took a step toward us, jumped back as a small wave washed over his feet, then shouted, "What is it you've found?" He waited. "You don't answer. Well, I'll find out or have you flogged, the both of you flogged."

For a time he stood looking after us, then began to walk back toward the mangroves. He would not find the chest that night and he would need to look hard in the daytime.

When we reached the ship I went straight to my brother's cabin. I found him on deck, his eyes fixed upon the sky. I had to speak to him twice before he heard me.

"It seems," he said, "that things are amiss above us. The heavens are paled o'er with a sickly look."

During the excitement of the past hour I had not noticed that the cloud bank, which earlier lay on the south horizon, had moved quickly up the sky and now had begun to overrun the moon.

"In such a way," Caleb said, "did the fateful storm come upon us. On such a night, after windless days and fearsome heat."

Hastily I told him about the chest I had found, all that had happened to it, and how Judd and I had just been threatened with a flogging. Caleb seemed not to hear me, at least he did not answer, as he kept his eyes on the fast-changing clouds.

"Aye, 'twas on such a night," he said and walked to the rail and back. "Couldst fate repeat itself and catch us once again? Couldst our good ship be wrecked as was the *Amy Foster*?"

Caleb gazed along the quiet deck. He raised his eyes and scanned the furled sails and the three bare masts. He glanced overhead at the racing clouds. Like something caged, he paced up and down, groaning to himself. It was clear that he wanted to take the ship out of the bay into the open sea, but some dark memory stirred his thoughts and held him back.

"Should we sail?" I said.

Caleb stopped his pacing and looked at me. "Aye," he replied. "We should have sailed an hour past."

"Then give the order," I said.

As if all this time he had been one of the crew waiting for a command, Caleb roused himself and said quietly, "Call the men."

I hurried to the forecastle, shouting as I went, and after a time awakened the crew. Mumbling, they staggered up the ladderway and were met on deck by an order to hoist the anchor and man the rigging, to bring in the tethered launches.

"Where hides the loutish Troll?" Caleb said to

me, casting a look toward the captain's empty station.

"On shore," I answered. "Remember that I told you we left him there."

"The ship shalt also leave him there," Caleb said. Cupping his hands to his mouth, he shouted aloft, "Full sail, hear me, full sail and break thy backs to do it."

The launches were hoisted on deck and fastened down. A light, copper-tasting wind now blew from the south. It caught the sails, the ship lay over and began to move slowly seaward, Caleb at the wheel.

I looked astern and though the moon was veiled saw a boat well out from shore, coming toward us. "Troll," I said and pointed.

Caleb made no move to change the ship's direction, but placed his feet apart and took a firmer hold upon the wheel. Looking off toward Rehusa Strait and the gathering clouds, my brother then said softly:

> "And now the Storm-Blast
>   came and he
> Was tyrannous and strong:
> He struck with his o'ertaking wings,
> And chased us west along.

With sloping masts and dipping prow
As who pursued with yell and blow
Still treads the shadow of his foe."

11

Between Isla Santa Margarita and Isla Creciente, lies the Strait of Rehusa, which leads by a twisting channel from the bay into the sea. The shores of the two islands are rocky, separated by shelving sand bars and little more than a ship's length of deep water.

" 'Twas here the *Amy Foster* went aground," Caleb said as we neared the strait. "We should take soundings by the lead. No time for that, alas. Thou at the main brace, whoever thou art, look sharp. Aye, struck down. We shall not be caught again."

The moon was hidden behind a sheath of pearly clouds. The Strait of Rehusa loomed hard off our starboard bow, its winding waters checkered black and gray from the moon's slanting light.

"No, not again," my brother said and spun the wheel to port. "She handles well, yet not so quick as

the *Amy*. A little sluggish in that respect, but mayhap
she knows her way to sea." He held the wheel with
one hand and cupped the other to shout aloft, "Mind
the fore-topmast staysail!"

Watching him, I could see despite the dangers
which lay before us, both in the narrow strait and
from the approaching storm, that he found this hour
greatly to his liking. Long months had passed since
he had stood at a ship's wheel or given a command,
often doubting that he ever would captain a ship
again. The glow of the binnacle lamp showed his
face set and grim, as it had been since that far day

in Nantucket, indeed, since first I remembered him.

Alert bore down the winding channel of Rehusa. She swung to port and then firm on a starboard tack and cleared the threatening shallows.

"She hath eyes," Caleb said.

But he spoke, I felt, more out of pride in himself than for the ship.

As we left Rehusa Strait and faced the first long waves of the open sea, my brother motioned me forward and put the wheel in my hands.

"Set thy feet square," he said. "Hold fast, 'tis a runaway chariot, pulled by a hundred rearing horses, thou guide now. Keep one eye upon the compass. The course reads westward—one eye upon the sails' set. Thy third eye keep upon the wind."

"I'd rather steer another time," I said, taking the wheel.

"The time is now," Caleb said. "Fair weather teacheth little. Thy father, rest his soul, was helmsman when bare seventeen, a captain at twenty-two. Aye, and his father before him. Stiffen thy knees whilst I go forward to cast a glance along the deck. 'Tis a tight ship we shall need ere morning dawns."

Suddenly I was alone with the heavy wheel. I

glanced at the compass resting in its pool of yellow light. The needle showed true west. I glanced at the sails, taut as if made of iron. I felt the living movement of the ship beneath my feet, as she lifted high and hung there a moment and ran down a long, long wave, and then slowly, slowly rose to meet another. I listened to the wind in the rigging and it was a different sound to me now than ever before. The salt spray that stung my face tasted different also. And when in a short time Caleb came to take the wheel, I handed it over reluctantly.

At three that morning, while the ship sped westward and the coast of Baja California lay safely astern, the chubasco struck. It drove us north for the rest of the day, our decks awash, and then through the night toward the east.

We huddled below the quarterdeck, crawling on hands and knees when we needed to move, all of us save Caleb, our captain. He stood at the wheel, lashed to it by a stout rope. Twice I crawled to him with a mug of water, which he drank, but he refused food. And as the second day dawned, with the fierce wind giving way to squalls of lightning and thunderous rain, he stood there still. His body bound to the wheel, his eyes never closing, he was like a lightning rod that draws off the storm's fury. He saved us all.

At noon or thereabouts the chubasco died away. The sails were set and we wore around and headed back for Magdalena. When we were through Rehusa Strait, Caleb called me aft.

"Take the storm-tossed ship," he said, "and bring her nigh the buoy which marks the *Amy Foster*. Aye, the buoy still floats there." He handed over the wheel. "Thou hast seen, Nathan, how she was lost, that fine ship, and how she might have lived had our brother Jeremy hearkened to my words."

12

THERE WAS no sign that a fierce chubasco had struck Magdalena. As the anchor went down and I lashed the wheel and looked around, everything was the same as I had seen it two short days before. The bay swept northward in a long, unbroken curve. To the east the endless marshes and their winding inlets lay unchanged under the hot sun. Nearer at hand, small waves wandered up the beach and beyond stood the mangroves, seemingly untouched.

But as I looked closer, hoping the chest had ridden out the storm, I saw something that made me jump. Against the rocks at the north end of the cove, strewn with kelp and pieces of brush, was a pile of splintered wood. For a while I stopped breathing; I then saw that a section of the wood was painted white and was marked in red with the two letters of a name. It was a boat from the *Alert,* the one Troll had taken.

In a moment, from a deep cave near the head of the cove, Troll appeared. He walked down the beach to the edge of the water and stood there, shading his eyes against the sun, staring out at the ship. I don't know who went over to pick him up or when, but I do know that he was there for supper, sitting by himself at the table near the galley door, and in the foulest of tempers.

Nor had his temper changed when we went out at dawn to dive again. He seated himself in the launch without a word, his shoulders hunched around his ears. When he did speak it was with a bite to his words.

My brother glanced at him now and again, and after an especially sharp command, which Troll shouted at Old Man Judd, cleared his throat. It is possible that he just remembered that the ship had sailed off and left Troll behind, alone on the island.

"Pouting art thou," he said. "For whatever reason? Oh yes, because we went to sea and saved thy ship. Whilst thou lived snugly upon the shore. What, tell me, wert thou about when the wind came and we needed thee aboard?"

Troll's ears grew red and he began biting his lips.

"What, tell me, wert thou about there on the shore," Caleb went on, "when we needed thee aboard? Stretching thy legs? Gathering seashells? Snooping out trouble? Whichever it was, Mr. Troll, henceforth give thy attention to the ship. Recall that this is the season of storms."

Afterward, Troll left off his shouting and for the rest of the day seemed in a better mood, at times, when my brother was around, even lighthearted. But at supper he left his food untouched and went above to pace the deck.

Judd and I decided that it was not wise to go to the cove that night, with Troll prowling up and down, on the watch for whatever we might do. There was a chance that he had found the chest. We agreed, however, that I should tell Caleb about it once more and ask his advice, which I did without delay.

"Thou think it a Spanish chest," Caleb said. I had found him again at the door of his cabin, looking across the water at the place where the *Amy Foster* lay. "Three paces in length and half as wide? Large for a chest, I'd say. Did thou tell me it hath the look of a canoe?"

"Yes, sometimes."

"Sometimes? When would that be? When thou has smelt a rum cork, mayhap."

"In certain lights," I said, "it looks like a canoe and in other lights like a chest."

"Hast seen it by light of day?"

"Yes."

"What doth it resemble then, chest or canoe?"

"Neither one, exactly. In the daylight it looks like a coffin."

"What dost thou say? A coffin?"

"Like Grandfather Caleb was buried in, the one with the big brass handles."

"Brass handles? A coffin? Thou must be joking, Nathan."

"It doesn't have brass handles," I said, "at least none I've seen. Also it looks like a canoe. I think it's a chest."

"Chest, canoe, coffin. Thou hast a choice there. Cradle to grave, aye, a wondrous choice."

"It has a lid, with long, square nails in it. More than a hundred."

"Then canst not be a canoe. Hast thou seen a lidded canoe, ever? No, nor I in all my worldly wanderings.

88

'Tis a monstrous thought, a lidded canoe, though the Esquimox hath one decked o'er save for a small hole wherein they sit."

Caleb paused, looking aloft where the tall spars swung to the tide and the waning moon wheeled westward. He ran a finger through his beard.

"Yet I do recall something from the book," he said. "Aye, it comes clearly now. 'Tis there on the hundreth page, more or less. Hast thou met a canoe in the book? Hast read this far?"

"Yes, beyond a chapter called 'The Doubloon.'"

"Doubloon! Aye, 'tis a thing I remember."

I likewise remembered it, for as I had read the scene where Captain Ahab nails the gold doubloon upon the mast there flashed before my eyes the time when Caleb had nailed the golden coins the Indians had given us. In my mind, the two scenes had become one — the three coins and the two strange men.

"But our thoughts fly afield," he said. "Back to the canoe. There's a fanciful part thou will soon overtake. Queequeg, the painted savage, thou hast met already, since he comes early. Thou wilt recall that this Queequeg was a native of Kokovoko, 'an island far away to the West and South,' and that he was the son of a King on his father's side and of unconquerable warriors on his mother's. Dost follow?"

"I remember Queequeg well."

"And thou wilt remember likewise that far along in the book, in chapter one hundred and ten, Queequeg is taken by a chill, which brought him to the very threshold. Whereupon they placed him in a hammock to die. But swinging there, while the rolling sea rocked him, he made a most curious request. Dost recall poor Queequeg's last request?"

"He asked them to build a coffin and put him in it, which they . . ."

"No, thou scamp things badly," my brother broke in. "It follows a fuller course. 'He called one of the crew to him and taking his hand, said that while in Nantucket he had chanced to see certain little canoes of dark wood, like the rich war-wood of his native isle, and upon inquiry, he had learned that all whalemen who died in Nantucket, were laid in those same dark canoes, and that the fancy of being so laid had much pleased him, for it was not unlike the custom of his own race, who, after embalming a dead warrior, stretched him out in his canoe, and so left him to be floated away to the starry archipelagoes.' "

"I remember."

"Aye, 'tis memorable. But tell me, hath the wood of this canoe-chest-coffin a darkish cast? Dost it remind thee somewhat of old, heathenish lumber hewn from aboriginal groves?"

"Whether it has a heathenish cast, I don't know. But it is a dark wood, almost black and very hard."

"Black it is and hard? Aye, it wouldst so appear, after countless suns have scorched it and seas tumbled it about, pickling it in brine."

My brother said no more and fell into a deep silence from which I made no effort to arouse him. I must confess that standing there as the moon cast shadows upon the deck and upon his white face, and the waves lapped softly at the ship, with a sound like that of people talking far away, I felt a cold hand upon my spine. And afterward while I lay reading in my bunk, the pages blurred and I could see only Caleb and not Ahab, and hear him talk, using words from the book I held before me.

13

We awakened to a cloudless sky and a breeze that drifted in from the west. Blue dolphins played around the ship. A flight of pelicans skimmed the bay, searching for small fish. Sea hawks searched the waters, too, and along the shore great turtles sunned themselves.

"A pretty day," Captain Troll said at breakfast, "the finest I've seen since we sailed to Magdalena."

Everyone agreed, glad to be alive, I suppose, after the storm, and thinking, no doubt, of the barrels of precious ambergris that still lay in the hold of the *Amy Foster*.

The Indians had survived the chubasco and sat waiting for us in their three canoes, beside the marker. To show good will, Caleb allowed the little chief to take a short turn at the pump. The chief appeared to be thankful for this gift, although the work was hard and

each time the heavy handle rose he rose with it and dangled in the air. He seemed happier, however, with the wheezing, whumping noises than with anything else.

Caleb had been down for about five minutes when I

noticed something that made my blood run cold. I had pushed on my end of the handle and the chief, clinging to his end, was in the air, a foot or so above the deck of the platform. As he came down, the breeze lifted his long hair and blew it from his face. I caught a glimpse of a bright gold ring fastened to his ear. I saw the ring for only an instant, but the band was broad and set with a large, green stone. It was the ring that had belonged to my brother Jeremy.

Saying nothing to the chief, I called Old Man Judd to help at the pump and when the chief had crawled back into his canoe, told him what I had seen.

Judd went on pumping for a time. "We'd better wait until Caleb's here," he said at last. "If we start a fight, there's no telling what will happen. The air hose might get fouled or the pump pushed overboard."

Caleb came to the surface at midmorning and as soon as he was out of his diving helmet, I told him about the ring. He took the news calmly.

" 'Tis ten of us against twenty of the savages," he said. "A poor bargain, they being armed with spears and heathenish arrows and we with nothing. Let's wait the morning. We'll meet them then with a brace of pistols."

"What if they disappear?" I said.

"Small chance of this," Caleb said, "while still there's treasure to be found. Aye, I recall the ring. 'Tis made of Inca gold and green turquoise mined by Aztecs. We shalt have it back."

We bolted on Caleb's helmet and he was ready to dive when a school of killer whales swam in. They came to prey upon the seals that were frolicking around our boats, watching us with their beautiful eyes as if there only to keep us company.

These mammoth black and white fish are shaped like fat torpedoes and weigh almost a ton, but they swim with great speed and slash about, using their teeth like razors. Their first rush drove the playful seals together, much as a herder herds his flock of sheep. With the gnashing of a thousand teeth, the killers set about the slaughter. As they left, the sharks sneaked in and began to cruise around, scavenging all that remained. Caleb, therefore, decided to quit for the day and sent all of the crew back to the ship, except Captain Troll, Judd and me.

"Hast seen the chest-coffin-canoe?" he said to Troll.

It was plain that Captain Troll had not, for his ears grew red and he began to stammer.

"Then thou hast no idea which canst be," my brother said, "canoe, coffin, chest?"

"I haven't seen anything," Troll said.

"Thou shalt see it now," my uncle said, "and tell truthfully what thou seest to the crew, lest they fear that we cheat them of something."

With proper tools, an ax, two chisels and a prying bar, we rowed ashore and made our way into the mangroves. The storm had scattered the brush that Judd and I had placed atop the chest, but the chest itself had not moved from its resting place in the deep mud.

At the first sight of it, Caleb drew in his breath, then took a step forward and placed a hand upon the smooth dark lid.

"Aye, as I thought," he said, "a heathenish color, war-wood hewn from the aboriginal groves of the Lackaday islands." He stepped back and passed a hand across his forehead. "But let's move it from this dismal place and set it rightly in the sun where we canst scan it better."

We pushed the heavy chest out of the mangroves and guided it through the water and shoved it up the beach. Judd and I set to work at once and chipped

away at the barnacles, while Caleb walked around the
chest and suveyed it from every side, talking to himself as he did so.

For most of an hour the old man and I worked,
while Troll stood aside and Caleb paced, never stop-
ping, never speaking save to hurry us on. At last, all
sides being cleaned, as we started chipping at the bot-

tom, Caleb said, "Leave the bottom be. These barnacles shall serve for ballast and keel to guide it straight upon a future voyage."

Whereupon he took up the prying bar and set to work upon the lid. He was as gentle as the old man had been, but still impatient.

"That gray builder of yore," he said, "set many a nail and deep. Yet 'tis good that he did, else it would not have lived through heaven's many storms, come sailing into us as fit a ship as poor Ishmael mounted when on that day the black bubble burst."

Having read the last page of *Moby-Dick: or, The Whale,* I understood my brother's words and why he had spoken them. Captain Troll did not, for he glanced at me and squinted his eyes in a knowing way.

The last nail came loose. Caleb grasped the lid and slowly raised it. The lid was heavy and taxed his strength, but he did not swing it aside nor let it fall. For a moment he stood cradling it in his arms, peering over it, down into the chest. Then he set the lid gently on the sand and came back and peered again into the chest, which, so far as I could see, was empty. Troll snickered. Judd and I were silent.

Caleb reached down and drew forth from the chest

a shriveled sea biscuit from among many that were ranged inside. Then he lifted out a large flask, which was sealed with wax, filled with a quantity of brackish water. He held both up for us to see, the square biscuit and the flask.

"Aye, the Canoe," he cried triumphantly, "the Dark Canoe. 'Tis as oft I've pictured it. As Queequeg ordered it built to send him safely to heaven's archipelagoes. As the old gray carpenter built it, of coffin-colored wood."

Silently Judd and I looked at each other, while Troll turned his head away and grinned.

Caleb put back the flask and biscuit, and taking up the lid, carefully placed it upon the chest.

"I'll make a further test, though none be needed," he said, running his hand along the lid's top edge. "Aye, 'tis certain proof. Come ye, feel the holes where the thirty Turk's heads were hung."

I stepped forward and dutifully felt the edge. As I did so, I remembered a scene from *Moby-Dick*. In it, Queequeg had recovered from his illness and had no further use for his coffin. Captain Ahab then ordered it sealed tight with pitch and oakum and made into a buoy. Also it was hung round with thirty pieces of rope, three feet long, each piece ending in a Turk's head knot, for use if the ship went down but the crew survived the killing of the great White Whale.

Troll and the old man did not step forward until my brother summoned them again. They then ran their hands along the edge, back and forth. There were a hundred and more holes from which the nails had been drawn, so they could say that a length of rope with a Turk's head knot might have hung there and there and there, which they did.

Caleb said no more, except to order the canoe pulled farther up the shore, out of reach of the tide. We rowed back to the ship in silence. It was a bad moment for the old man and me, for we had thought to the last that our work would be rewarded by a glittering horde of Spanish gold. But Caleb's silence was not ours. He sat in a trance, his eyes wildly staring, as if he had just found the world's richest treasure.

14

Armed with a brace of pistols that belonged to Captain Troll, we rowed up to the marker at dawn. The Indian chief and his followers were nowhere in sight, so the weapons were hidden away and we made ready for Caleb to dive.

As soon as the pump began to groan and wheeze, the Indians came gliding over the calm water from the direction of Isla Ballena. The little chief climbed out of his canoe and onto the diving platform and smiled, waiting for Caleb to invite him to take over the pump. Instead, Troll pressed a pistol against his chest.

The chief no doubt was surprised, for he made no effort to defend himself. His followers, however, instantly paddled away, beyond range of the pistols (apparently they had seen one before) and brandished their spears.

Troll wished to kill the chief without further ado. "The only good Indian," he said, "died long ago."

Caleb made no reply to this suggestion, but took hold of the chief's hair, which fell to his shoulders, and pulled it back. The ring hung from his ear, held there by a hook fashioned from a piece of seashell. Caleb snatched it away.

The chief looked at the ring and then at Caleb. He seemed more surprised than outraged at what had happened to him, until Caleb put the ring on his own finger and began to make signs. It was not good sign language that Caleb spoke, but at last the chief understood and spoke back.

He jumped in the water, turned over on his back, and closed his eyes, which we understood to be a dead man floating. Then he climbed into the launch and pointed down the bay, in the direction of Isla Ballena.

It was plain from his actions that the little chief meant us to believe that he had found Jeremy's body floating somewhere in the bay.

"He's lying," Troll shouted. "He goes around with a dead man's ring in his ear and wants us to think he found it."

Glancing at the little chief and then at Troll, my

brother seemed to make up his mind. He fished in his pocket and took out the ring. As he turned it over in the palm of his hand, there came back to me the time long ago when he had brought back to Nantucket, after a year-long voyage, the beautiful green stone and the rough piece of Inca gold. I recalled that he had asked Smith the jeweler to make them into a ring to fit my father's finger. I suppose, looking at the ring now, he remembered that when Jeremy had sailed off on his first voyage our father had given the ring to him, his favorite son, as a token of good fortune.

Whether or not Caleb believed the little chief's story, I had no way of telling. Perhaps he had his own idea of who the murderer was. Perhaps he thought, as I did, that it was Captain Troll. Whatever it may have been, suddenly he placed the ring in the chief's hand and pointed to the pump.

Chief Bonsig beamed, placed the ring carefully in his ear, and grasped the pump handle. As it began to move up and down, the other Indians came back and clustered around the launch.

"There are waters under waters," Caleb said. "But know ye, there is only one righteous God and He is Lord over the earth."

Was Caleb saying that at last, after many long years, by the gift of the ring to the little chief he had settled a carking score with his brother Jeremy? I am not certain. For only a moment later, glancing at me, he said:

"The Assyrian came down like the wolf on the fold,
And his cohorts were gleaming in purple and gold;
And the sheen of their spears was like stars on the sea,
When the blue wave rolls nightly on deep Galilee."

15

I SLEPT little that night, going over in my mind the story Chief Bonsig had acted out for us. There was only a small chance that Jeremy's body had survived in the unfriendly waters of Magdalena Bay, waters that teemed with all forms of ravenous life. But small as the chance was, I decided to take it.

Before sunrise the old man and I left the ship and rowed off toward Isla Ballena. We were not even sure that the Indians lived on the island, although each morning they paddled in from that direction.

The rising sun shone in our eyes and we were close upon Ballena before I could see it clearly. At first glance, like all the islands of the bay, it seemed barren, little more than a nesting place for birds. But as we approached a spit near its eastern shore, a crescent-shaped beach came into view. A few palms fringed

the beach, a narrow, wooded valley lay beyond, and a winding path that ended against a cliff. There were no canoes on the beach or other signs of life, yet it was a likely spot for a village. We rowed toward it.

Without warning, as we came abreast of the spit, our boat was seized by a churning tide that lifted the bow and drove us instantly astern, like a cork blown from the neck of a bottle. We bumped and twisted, scarcely touching the water, for a quarter of a mile or so, until the channel widened into the bay and the raging current lost its force.

"We'll have to wait for the tide to turn," I said.

"It may be a long wait," Judd replied.

"We could go ashore and walk along the shore. We might be able to reach the valley that way."

"We would have to climb the cliff," the old man said, pointing to a headland that rose steeply out of the bay. "Let's wait. The longer we're here the less time we'll have to work over there at the wreck. And maybe the Indians will come along. It's about time."

We waited more than two hours for slack tide, and when the Indians did not appear, entered the channel and without further trouble made in toward the beach. Wisps of smoke rose from a grove of trees and I heard the sound of voices and the laughter of children at play.

"It's not a good idea to land before we're invited," the old man said, resting on his oars. "Chief Bonsig was happy when he left us yesterday, but the fact that he hasn't gone back this morning is sort of suspicious."

"He may remember that Troll wanted to shoot him," I said.

While we were talking, dogs began to bark and a moment later a swarm of Indians burst from the trees, as if we had upset a hive. Behind them trotted Chief

Bonsig, who motioned us to land and even waded out to help slide the boat up the beach.

He beamed, smiling his toothless smile, and made a sweeping gesture that took in the channel, the shore, and the wooded valley. He then pointed admiringly at himself. I understood why he felt proud of his island kingdom, for it seemed to possess wood for fire, water to drink, and a plentiful supply of food near at hand. Above all, the fierce tide that ran between the island and the coast, through an opening no more than a hundred yards in width, would make his village very difficult to attack.

Judd and I let him know how much we liked his island. By signs I then told him why we had come. He either didn't understand me or chose not to. Jabbering away in his harsh dialect, which sounded like rocks rattling around inside a barrel, he waved his warriors aside and led us into a grove.

We soon came to a cleared space, in front of a deep wide-mouthed cave. A fire was burning under a big pot and we gathered around it, while the warriors went off among the trees to watch us. Chief Bonsig laid out three bowls of stew, which Judd said was made of dog meat. We both ate little.

As my eyes became used to the darkness of the grove, I saw that the cave I was facing was lined with crude statues cut deeply into the stone. They were fashioned in the shape of men with arms folded upon their chests, shell beads around their necks, and bits of gold, which shone in the firelight, for eyes.

I pointed to the figures and then watched while the little chief made a sign that I took to mean a time long ago, and more signs that could have meant that all the stone men were his ancestors. When he had finished, peering deeper into the cave, I saw that against the walls were three or four different figures. The light was poor, but they looked like the forms of Spanish soldiers, standing upright, clothed in doublets, breastplates, and steel helmets.

As I continued to stare into the dim recesses of the cave, scarcely believing my eyes, the little chief jumped to his feet, called to his warriors, and led us quickly out of the grove to the beach. There I again asked him for the body of my brother. Once more he went through his motions of the previous day, lying on the sand and pointing to the tide that rushed through the channel.

Judd, while the little chief was doing this, spoke to

me twice. The second time I glanced at him, struck more by the tone of his voice than by what he had said. His eyes were fixed on a stony shelf not more than a dozen paces from where we stood. A lone tree grew there on the shelf, its thin branches weirdly warped by the wind. Beneath the tree, on a platform of carved wood inlaid with triangles and squares of abalone shell, half hidden among the scanty leaves, lay the body of my brother Jeremy. So real was his appearance, so lifelike, I could not believe that he was dead. He could have climbed to the ledge on a summer day and there fallen asleep.

I had read of Indian tribes who, instead of burying their dead, in some secret manner embalmed them and set them away in trees or caves or upon stone cairns. I also had read of Indians who worshiped as gods men with blond hair, which must have been the custom with this tribe. For when I approached the ledge and grasped one of the handholds cut into its face, Chief Bonsig, flanked by his men, held me back.

I pulled away and confronted him, but a warning from Judd brought me to my senses.

"Act as though you think it's proper for Jeremy to be lying up there," he said quietly. "Don't forget, we're outnumbered."

Taking Judd's advice, I made signs that I was pleased and walked off. We both got in the boat and waited for the tide to slacken. It was a long wait. Chief Bonsig left six of his men to stand guard beside the ledge and with the rest disappeared into the grove. Now and again, as we sat waiting, I saw faces peering out at us from the trees.

What fears we had proved groundless. For when

the tide changed, the little chief came bouncing down to the shore and stood waving until we were out of sight. We rowed hard, however, long after we were out of the channel.

"I believe the chief's story," Judd said, speaking for the first time since we left the island. "I think he did find Jeremy's body floating around in the channel."

"But how did it get there?" I asked.

"On the tide, most likely. He must have gone to the island for some reason."

"He must have used a boat then. On the morning he disappeared, none of our boats was missing. All of them were moored at the ship's stern."

Judd lit his pipe and sucked away at it for a while. "That's true, I saw them myself. But what if Jeremy went off to the island with Blanton or Troll or one of the other men?"

"For what reason?"

"I don't know, but let's say that he did. Say there were two of them in the boat and they got caught in the tide like we did. Say that your brother got thrown out and drowned and the other man, whoever it was, rowed back to the ship. Wouldn't that explain why none of the boats was missing?"

"Yes it would. But who was the other man? Why didn't he tell us what happened? It wasn't his fault if the boat got caught in the tide and Jeremy was drowned. He couldn't be blamed for an accident."

Judd picked up his oar and we set off toward the wreck of the *Amy Foster*.

"Well, whoever it was," Judd said, "he felt real guilty about something."

16

It was well past noon as we wearily rowed up to the *Amy Foster*.

Blacksmith Grimes, who liked to display his strength, was alone at the pump. The rest of the crew sat around in the launches, with their eyes fixed upon the signal line. Captain Troll held it in his hand as if he were waiting for a fish to bite. He knew where we had been, but since he didn't ask what had happened to us we did not bother to tell him.

About an hour later, he jumped to his feet and shouted, acting exactly like a man who has been fishing all day without luck and then suddenly hooks into a monster. Caleb had signaled for the chain and grapple.

The crew cheered as the grapple descended. In silence they waited for the signal to haul in. When it came they began to count their share of the ambergris and make plans for the future. Grimes said he would leave the sea, and good riddance, get a soft rocking chair, and sit on the porch and watch the ships leave Nantucket harbor. Blanton had a farm in mind where he could raise ducks. Greene did not like ducks, but he did like Toggenburg goats. Everyone had a plan of some sort.

As for myself, I watched the line slowly come in, but I did not expect another cask of ambergris. I knew that the grapple held in its claws something far different. I knew because Caleb had told me after the second cask was found that he was going to search only for the log of the *Amy Foster*.

The claws held a small iron box, much like the one in which my mother once had stored nutmegs, cloves, and other spices from the Indies. Troll unhooked the box and flung it down upon the platform, with the look of a fisherman who expects a toothsome sole at the end of his line and finds instead a bony skate. The crew stared.

After a short while my brother came to the surface. The first thing he did when we removed his diving suit was to look anxiously around for the iron box, as if he thought it might have taken wings and flown away. It sat at his feet, rusty and streaked with mud. Judd handed him a bar to pry the lid, but he refused it, and, gathering the box in his arms, asked me to row him to the ship.

The big white cat met us at the door of the cabin, pleading for food which for some reason it always needed. Caleb gently brushed it aside, picked his way through the clutter of books, and set the box on the chart table. Though the cabin was not dark, he asked me to light the lantern. I thought then that he was ready to open the box and went off to fetch a hammer.

When I returned he was standing at a porthole, his eyes fixed upon the distant sea. Impatient, I struck the iron box a blow with the hammer and asked if now he wished it opened. He slowly turned, passing a hand across his forehead. He gave me a look of desperation, as if he feared to know what lay inside, as if on that day of approaching storm he might not have written a command, after all.

At last, when he did not speak nor move, I swung open the lid and took out the log of the *Amy Foster*. It was a small book bound in leather, half the size of the iron box, soaked through by the sea, the edges

curled and stuck together. It was more like a lump of
dough than a ship's log.

I held it out to him, but so great was his excitement
that the book fell from his grasp.

"Thou canst do what is needed," he said. "Thou

hast steadier hands and eyes that art less fearful than mine."

I placed the logbook on the table, and without knowing if I were doing the right thing slipped the blade of a penknife lying at hand between the pages of a small section. The paper was of a fine linen make and inch by inch came apart.

Caleb seized the pages from my hand and searched them for a date. " 'Tis the tenth of August I have here. It lies farther along. The twenty-first of September, if I recall."

While Caleb watched over my shoulder, I started over again. The next pages I pried loose held an entry for September first. At this time Caleb left me to pace the deck. The following entry was for five days later, but so dimmed by water that it scarcely could be read.

I was seized by the thought that the final page, if ever I came to it, the page that Caleb was pacing the deck about, might be damaged beyond reading. Always before, I had secretly hoped that the log would never be found, for if what Caleb had said was true, then my brother Jeremy had lied to the board of inquiry, to everyone, to me.

The logbook lay open on the table, the last pages waiting for the sharp blade of the knife. It would be a simple matter to destroy them. I confess that I stood there, thinking. The ship's three clocks struck the hour of five. The clocks were not in time with each other and their bells went on ringing for a long while. I heard Caleb's steps on the deck, moving back and forth, the bump, bump of his good foot, the soft, dragging slide of the other.

Yet it was not from any real concern for Caleb that I unloosened the last page with the greatest of care. Nor was it from pity. It was the knowledge that if I did destroy the writing there before me, I would never know whether or not my brother Jeremy had solemnly lied to the board of inquiry, lied because he had wilfully disobeyed a command, lied to save himself.

Setting the page down, I called to Caleb. He hobbled slowly in from the deck, as if now that the moment had come he feared to face it. He lifted the lantern from its hook overhead and held it close. His body was shaking and the light wavered back and forth. I took the lantern from him.

The writing was in his hand, large and with a for-

119

ward, headlong slant to the words. We read them together, I to myself, Caleb aloud in his quiet, far-off voice.

" 'September twenty-first,' " he read. " 'The southern storm approacheth. Do not be caught in Magdalena. Take the ship to sea. Heed thou my command, Jeremy, take the ship to sea. Thou shalt . . .' "

The sentence ended abruptly. The last word was scrawled across the page as if at that instant Caleb had dropped the pen.

" 'Thou shalt,' " Caleb said, slowly repeating the final words. " 'Tis unfinished. Yet enough. Whilst the fever raged, still did I give the command. Aye, 'tis plain, 'tis plain that I did give it."

Caleb set the lantern back on its hook and gazed down at me. I waited for him to say a word or give some sign of rejoicing. He had come five thousand leagues and searched for weeks to learn if he had given this command or if instead he had only dreamed it. On that morning in Nantucket, saying not a word as they stripped him of his captain's license, he did not know. But now at last the log sat there on the table for all to see.

I waited. The cabin was quiet, save for the big white

cat who lay purring on a pile of books, and the creaking of timbers as the ship rose and fell to the movement of the tide. Silently Caleb looked down at me. Perhaps he felt that his long search had been for nothing, now that Jeremy was dead. Perhaps this was the same sad moment for him, despite the years of hatred between them, that it was for me.

17

THERE WAS no answer when I knocked on Caleb's door early the next morning. But Sapphire was crying for food, so I went in and fed him part of my brother's breakfast.

The lantern had burned through the night, and having guttered low, was filling the cabin with streamers of gray smoke. I turned it off and set it aside to take below. On the chart lay the lumpish pages of the log, now bound together with a piece of heavy twine. Caleb was asleep, lying on his bunk fully clothed, as if he had fallen there in a moment of deep exhaustion.

I gave Sapphire the rest of Caleb's breakfast to keep him quiet and picked up the lantern. As I tiptoed to the door and glanced back to see if the sounds had awakened my brother, I was struck by something I had not noticed before.

Summers in Nantucket when the family went to the shore to swim, Caleb never came along. And aboard ship at times when everyone dove from the deck or rowed ashore to swim, he stayed in his cabin. For that reason I had never until this moment seen the twisted leg he hobbled around on. Now, as he lay sprawled across the bunk with one trouser leg pulled up, the long, twisting wound was exposed.

I closed the door quietly behind me, feeling that I had seen something I should not have seen. And yet, as I walked down the deck trying to blot it from my mind, the scene in the cabin persisted. I then realized that I wanted it to, that for the first time in my life I had seen my brother whole. Always before he had been an object to fear and to pity, but never someone, a human being, who could be liked and perhaps loved.

The news I brought to the forecastle was a surprise. When I told Captain Troll and the crew that Caleb was asleep, everyone began to grumble. Troll paused with a spoon of mush halfway to his mouth.

"Asleep," he said, "with all that ambergris waiting out there?"

"Winter's coming," Blanton put in. "You can't dive with the wind blowing fits and waves running."

Troll shoved the mush into his mouth. "Asleep," he said. "Clegg's asleep!"

I went into the galley and got my breakfast and brought it back to the table.

"Caleb Clegg's asleep," I said, "because he's tired. For a month now he's been the first on deck in the morning and the last to go to bed. He found the ambergris. You have two casks of it. Another morning or even another day won't make any difference to any of you."

Troll jabbed the table with his spoon. He puckered his smooth, pink face and was about to say something in reply when Tom Waite walked in.

"Nathan's right," he said. "Let Caleb sleep if he wants to."

Tom went up the ladderway, motioning us to follow, and we manned the launches and rowed over to the *Amy Foster*. It was hard work getting Tom into the diving suit because his arm still pained him. But once the helmet was bolted on, he slipped over the side and sank with a wave of his hand, graceful as a frisking dolphin.

An hour or more passed while the pump wheezed

and rattled, sending air into the depths, and Tom's breaths came floating back to us in a chain of bright bubbles. Then the first signal came on the line, but not for the grapnel hook. It was a signal to pull Tom in.

"What's down there?" Troll asked, trying to speak calmly, as soon as Tom's helmet was off. "How much ambergris? Ten casks? Twenty? Sit down. That's it, take your time and get a good breath. What's your guess? Tweny-five casks?"

After a while Tom got to his feet, took a deep breath, and glanced down at the wavering outlines of the sunken ship.

"Thirty?" Troll said.

"Nothing," Tom answered. "I didn't find one cask of ambergris. And the sperm oil is beginning to float. Every cask I saw was breached."

Troll took off his square-crowned hat and mopped his brow. He stared at Tom.

"Breached?" he said. "You saw no ambergris?"

Tom nodded. "If there's ambergris down there, it's hidden deep. We'd have to haul every barrel to find it. And there's not enough good oil to fill a lamp."

Troll glared down into the water. "Things are becoming clear," he said, his voice rising to an angry whine. "Little wonder that Clegg's asleep."

Taking a quick step forward, he gave the helmet a swipe with his foot, then a kick that sent it tumbling overboard. He watched the helmet slide away from the launch and sink. Again he wiped his brow.

"Man the boats," he shouted. "We're finished with the *Amy Foster*."

18

THE SHIP was quiet the rest of the morning. Troll sent off three men to fill the water casks and three to hunt geese in the marshes. The rest of us he ordered into the rigging with tar pail and brush. Troll gave no reasons, but it seemed that he was getting the ship ready to sail.

About noon Caleb appeared in the galley and asked for a cup of coffee. A short time later, Captain Troll came down the ladder. You could never be sure how Troll felt, except that when he was in one of his bad moods a thin smile often lurked around the corners of his mouth. The smile was there as he spoke to my brother.

"I guess we'll be sailing anytime," he said, "now that we've found all the ambergris."

Caleb looked at Troll over the rim of his cup. "How dost thou know that all hath been found?"

"While you were asleep this morning," Troll replied, "Tom Waite made a long dive. That's how I know, Mr. Clegg."

Caleb finished his coffee and put his cup on the table. "Tom is a fine diver, whilst I am poor," he said. "Thou canst trust him about all things that lie beneath the sea."

Troll for a moment seemed to be taken aback by my brother's willingness to believe Tom Waite. The thin smile around his mouth grew thinner.

"Tom also reported that the barrels are breached," Troll said. "Oil is leaking everywhere."

"Yes, I have noted this," Caleb said. "On my last dive. 'Tis a bad sign, yet some good oil must remain."

"If any does," Troll answered quickly, "it will take a month to haul it out, Tom tells me."

"Aye, a month, yet canst be done if all turn a hand," Caleb said. "Dost wish to search or sail? 'Tis for thee to choose."

Captain Troll walked to the ladderway, glanced above at the hot sky, came back and thrust his feet apart.

"I choose to sail," he said. "I've already sent men for supplies. We can sail before nightfall."

"Nightfall?" said Caleb. " 'Tis too soon, Mr. Troll. There are certain things that must be done ere we sail."

"Well, let's do them," Troll said.

"No, 'tis something thou canst not do. Thou hast a practical turn of mind, Mr. Troll. What's needed here is the impractical. More the flighty sort, so to speak, that sees the bone beneath the flesh, the star behind the cloud."

Troll glanced at me as if he thought I would know what Caleb was talking about. Disappointed, he came to a decision. At least he set his hat squarely upon his head, walked with measured steps to the ladderway, and disappeared above.

I should have known what Caleb meant to do. Since the log had been found and he had little interest in trying to recover Jeremy's body, there really was only one project left for him. But I did not know until he sent me flying off to fetch Old Man Judd that he meant to do something with his canoe.

"Gather thy best tools," he told the old man, "and thy sharpest nails. No bent ones, mind thee, none drawn hastily from common wood for we undertake a most uncommon task. Likewise gather a goodly length of oakum and a brimming pot of pitch for we shalt require them."

Judd did as he was told and within the hour we set out for the cove. The canoe was where we had left it, high above the tide, its odd-shaped lid, the packet of sea biscuits and flask of water lying nearby.

With his hands clasped at his back and his head cocked to one side, Caleb strolled around the canoe — stalked is perhaps the better word — studying it from all angles, saying to himself, "Aye, 'tis the dark canoe, which comforted Queequeg as he lay upon the brink and in time bore good Ishmael safely homeward. Aye, 'tis the one, the one."

Not until he had made a dozen circuits of the canoe did he turn to Judd. "Now where wouldst thou begin?" he asked. "Not from the beginning for it hath already a shape given by a master hand, proven seaworthy by the years and circumstance. What say about this, Judd?"

Thinking no doubt of Nantucket, Judd was for nailing the lid on at once.

Caleb looked askance, shook his shaggy head. "Nay,

130

thy haste confounds me. Back the mainsail and plot
a different course. Toward the north, Judd, the true,
polar north."

"What?" said Judd. "What do you aim to do with
it?"

"Hast thou not been told already?" Caleb said, as
though to a half-bright child. "To sail, Judd, upon the
sea, the sea that lies beyond yon headland. This first.
Then upon the airier seas that foam and swirl within
the mind."

"Well," said Judd, "if such is the case we best had
smooth her down a bit."

"Aye, use a cautious hand. There's only one of this.
Thou canst not make another should you try from

now into eternity. Take care. Thinkest twice before thou unloose thy skills."

With a slight shrug, Judd thought for a while. Then of a sudden, somehow caught up in the spirit of the task, he set to work. He worked slowly, as he had before when together we had removed the lid, filled the nail holes with putty and planed all edges satin-smooth.

"Canst tie a Turk's head," Caleb asked while we were rowing back to the ship at sundown, "the size to fit a grasping hand?"

"No," I said, "but I can tie a bowline."

"A good knot, but 'tis cumbersome to the eye. Judd, canst thou tie the Turk's head? Aye, so I thought. Thou hast tied many in thy day. Then have for me in the morning early fifteen such knots. I myself shalt tie the rest. Nathan here can lend a hand. Tom Waite also. And mind ye, line of the best quality, an arm in length, the bitter end worked with pitch, the other in a fulsome Turk's head."

19

AFTER SUPPER Judd collected materials for Caleb's thirty knots and I persuaded Tom Waite to help with the tying. The three of us took ourselves to the far stern of the ship, where we would not have to listen to the jibes of the crew, and set to work by the glow of a small lantern and a waning moon. Tom and the old man wove the intricate knots, while I cut the line to the length Caleb had demanded and bound the loose ends with stout linen thread.

We were still working away when the ship's three clocks struck midnight. From time to time during the past hour, I had caught glimpses of Captain Troll pacing the foredeck, pausing to look over the side at the star-flecked water, or from the shadows to cast an eye in our direction.

At the sound of the bells he came sauntering aft.

The night was hot and he stopped for a drink at the water cask. He climbed the ladder and took up a place outside the circle of our lantern.

"I suppose," he said, glancing down at the row of finished lines I had laid out on deck, "I suppose all this knot-tying has to do with that thing you fished out of the bay. You're wasting good hemp, that's what you're doing."

His voice rose as he spoke. My brother's cabin was just below us and the door was open. I wondered if Troll wasn't speaking to him instead of to us.

"You're wasting good time, too," he went on, "holding up the ship that's all ready to sail." He walked over to the binnacle, glanced at the compass as if he were steering the ship at sea, then stood for a moment at the head of the ladder, staring at us. "If you ask me," he said, "you're a pack of fools."

The three of us said nothing and he went down the ladder, softly whistling to himself.

"I don't know how you feel," Tom said when Troll was out of earshot, "but I think we *are* a pack of fools. Who else but a fool would sit here on his haunches for five hours and tie knots. Turk's heads at that. Why not something simple like a Granny."

"A Granny wouldn't look proper," said Judd, sounding a little like Caleb.

Tom stood up and walked around the binnacle to stretch his legs and sat down again.

"This whole thing puzzles me," he said. "Why thirty knots. What's the idea, anyway?"

135

"That's how it is in the book," I explained.

"What book?" Tom asked.

Moby-Dick: or, The Whale," I said.

"What's *Moby-Dick* got to do with it?"

"Everything," I said.

Before I could say more, Tom rose without a word and went down the ladderway. For a time I heard him talking to Captain Troll.

"Thirty nails stuck up about half an inch all around the lid," Judd mused.

"As if something had been fastened to them once," I said.

"And then rotted away in the sea."

"Strips of wood could have been nailed to the lid."

"All the wood wouldn't have rotted. Some would be left," the old man said. "The nails must have been fastened down with thirty lengths of Manila line. Manila doesn't last long in the water."

The gray fog quietly swept past us, leaving the sky clear and aswarm with stars. In the dim light of our lantern we looked long at each other.

"Does the book say anything more?" the old man asked me at last.

136

I thought for a while, going back over all that I had read about the dark canoe. "Yes, there was something else," I said. "After Queequeg decided not to die, he used his coffin for a sea chest and emptied into it his canvas bag of clothes. In his spare time he then carved the lid with all kinds of odd figures. They were copied from the tattoos on his body, which had been put there by a prophet who lived on the island where Queequeg was born. These odd figures gave the complete story of the heavens and the earth and also told how to find the truth about all things. Queequeg made the carvings before Ahab ordered the coffin made into a life buoy, but the carpenter probably left them there when he worked on the lid."

The old man pulled at his lower lip. "I remember, I remember," he said in a voice so low I could scarcely hear him. "Strange looking, they were. I took them for the borings of sea worms and planed them out, every one of them. Carvings, you say, made by a prophet?"

"Likely, you're right, thinking they were made by sea worms."

The old man slowly shook his head. "No, too regular for worms, now that I think about it. Sort of geometrical. More like drawings, drawings on an Egypt tomb. Hieroglyphical, so to speak."

The old man got to his feet and bundled up the lines we had made that night. For a time we stood by the binnacle, looking off toward the cove where small waves left trails of phosphorescence and the dark canoe lay.

"All this is against nature, unnatural, if you ask me," the old man said. "But strange things go on. Once — it was before you were born — I was sailing through Sundra Strait. A night just like this, with more stars in the sky than fish in the sea. I was at the wheel, thinking we might do with a mite more sail. Of a sudden, right there, right in the middle of the mainsail, I saw a face. It was my mother's face, but all out of shape as though she was crying and calling out to me. That night was the fourth of August and I recall the hour because I had just gone on watch. Three months later to the day, back in Nantucket, the first news I heard when I stepped ashore was the word that my mother had died. Died on the fourth of August, at the very time of night I stood there at the wheel and saw her face, as plain, Nathan, as I see yours. Yes, strange things do go on about us."

Listening to the old man's words, while an unseen tide tugged at the ship and set its timbers to creaking softly, as the great constellations silently wheeled over our heads, I more than half believed him.

20

CALEB FINISHED his share of the Turk's head knots, toiling at them all night, and around noon the three of us started off for the cove. Captain Troll and the crew watched us leave. Standing at the rail they sent us off with a shower of catcalls and jeers. Tom Waite, who was the only man at work, paused high in the rigging and with his tar brush made a circle in the air, then pointed at his head to let us know that, like Troll, he thought us a pack of fools.

In the light of day with the sun bearing down upon us, Caleb sitting in the stern with his hair wildly blowing in the hot wind, his arms full of Turk's head knots, I could not blame him much.

Nor did I feel differently when we reached the lifebuoy.

"Keep thy wits about thee," he cautioned us. "She is to be fair to the eye, as on that fateful day when the White Whales set her adrift in southern seas."

After about two hours of work, the lid was ready to fasten down. But then, as Judd set it in place and started to drive the first nail, Caleb remembered that his dark canoe lacked a new packet of biscuits and a flask of fresh water. I was sent back to the ship, therefore, to fetch them.

Tom Waite was still in the rigging, along with the rest of the crew. As I climbed over the rail, he paused and again made a circle in the air and pointed to his head. There were also some scattered calls from the crew.

I went to the galley posthaste, filled the flask, wrapped a dozen biscuits in a piece of oil cloth, and was at the bottom of the ladderway when I saw Captain Troll standing above me. I stepped aside and he came slowly down.

"How long is your brother going to putter around out there?" he said. "All day?"

"Perhaps longer," I replied. "They're just beginning to nail on the lid. There are lines to fasten and seams to caulk. I don't know what else."

"Looks like another day of it," said Troll. He turned, glanced up the ladderway, and listened for a moment. "When you were over on the island, the time you found Jeremy's body, did you by any chance see gold lying around? A chest or anything like that?"

"No."

"Did you look?"

"I didn't think to."

"The chief had a whole bag of gold coins when he came to the ship. Remember? There must be more where they came from."

Steps sounded above us and two of the men stopped for a drink at the water cask. Troll waited until they had finished and walked on.

"You know the way to the island," he said. "Besides, the chief and you are friends since Caleb gave him the ring. I was thinking we could row over and have a look around. Pay them a friendly visit. Just the two of us. If we find gold there's no sense in dividing it up, is there?"

Suddenly, as I listened to Troll, I had a strong suspicion that it was he who had gone to the island with my brother on the day Jeremy drowned.

"You'll be helping over at the cove the rest of the afternoon," he said. "But that don't matter. The tide won't be changing for three hours yet."

"The tide?" I said. "What has the tide to do with it?"

Troll stood in the dim light that came down the ladderway. I watched his eyes shift away from me and back again.

"I hear there's a bad one between the island and the coast," he said. "Strong enough to capsize a good-sized boat."

"And it did capsize a boat," I replied, "the boat Jeremy was in."

Troll was surprised by my words. At least he was silent for a while, thinking about them. But at that moment I doubt that he cared whether or not I knew that he had been with Jeremy on that morning. His mind had fastened upon the Indian gold.

"When we're over there," he said, in a further effort to interest me in the plan, "we'll bring Jeremy back."

"It would take every man in the crew and every gun we own. They worship him. They think more of him than their gold."

"You may be right," Troll said. "We'll go over first and look around."

He slipped past me, quietly climbed the ladder,

glanced fore and aft along the deck, and came quickly back.

"There's a lot of big ears around," he explained, lowering his voice. "You said that the Indians think more of Jeremy than they do their gold. I take it that you saw some of it sitting around."

"I saw a little," I said, angry at myself for having mentioned gold at all.

"How much?"

I said nothing and Troll stood for a moment staring at me, not waiting for me to answer, but lost in some wild dream that made his thin mouth quiver.

"The tide turns in about three hours," he said. "Take the stuff back to Caleb and then leave. Tell him I need you here. An important matter. That will give us time to reach Isla Ballena when the tide's right."

"I can't get away."

Troll ran his tongue over his lips. "You can't get away?" he said. "Why? Because you blame me for your brother's death? Well, get it through your head that it was his idea from the first. Not mine. I never thought of going over there for the Indians' gold until he brought it up."

144

"No, I don't blame you for Jeremy's death. But I do blame you for not telling us what happened to him. Why didn't you? Was it because you planned to go back to the island again? By yourself this time, so you wouldn't have to share what you stole with someone else?"

Troll blinked. He started to speak and stopped after mumbling one word. I waited for him to go on, but there was no need to, for I could see by the confused look on his face that I had already answered for him. Turning away, I went up the ladder.

"Be back in an hour," he shouted, suddenly regaining his voice. "If you're not, I'll give the order to sail. I'll leave you over there in the cove. You and your brother and Old Man Judd, too. Maybe you and your crazy brother would like that. Since you've got a good life buoy with thirty handholds hanging on it, and an armful of provisions, you can all sail to Nantucket or somewhere."

I untied the launch and rowed off to the cove. I told Caleb about Captain Troll's threat as soon as I waded ashore. He was driving one of the big square nails. He did not even look up.

21

THE SEA BISCUITS and the flask of water were stowed away in the life buoy and carefully roped so they would not roll around. The lid was nailed, the seams caulked tight with oakum and pitch, the thirty Turk's head knots, beautiful to behold in their intricate weaving, fastened to the six sides of the lid with long, square nails, new as the day they came from the foundry.

Throughout the blazing afternoon, I kept a close eye upon the ship. But so far as I could tell, Caleb never glanced at her once. He knew Captain Troll better than I did.

The last nail was driven at sundown and on a neap tide we pushed the life buoy, which Caleb called the dark canoe, down the sloping shore. It floated high in the water, now that all the barnacles had been scraped off save those that covered the bottom, on an even keel like the best of the little Nantucket boats. And like a boat we towed it back to the ship and moored it at the stern.

We would have sailed that hour on the turning tide, with a good breeze at our backs, except that Captain Troll was not on board. He had rowed off soon after I had left the ship, Tom Waite told us, in the direction of Isla Ballena, saying that he would return around midnight.

At midnight, as I went on watch, he had not returned, nor did he appear at dawn. When noon came and he still was missing, Caleb sent three of us — Judd, Tom Waite, and me — to search for him on Ballena and in the waters nearby.

We were unable to reach the island because of the heavy current, but close to nightfall, as we were about to give up the search, Tom Waite spotted Troll's wrecked boat, wedged in a crevice of the rocky headland. Troll we never found, though we went back the next morning, searched once more, and asked Chief Bonsig about him.

With a thumb and four fingers, the little chief made the sign of a jaw, a shark's jaw I presumed, then rapidly opened and closed his hand to describe Troll's fate. My brother's body I saw again, lying there on the headland. Tom Waite wanted to risk his life to carry it away, but Judd and I persuaded him not to.

When we reached the ship I found Caleb at once and gave him the news of Troll's death. He was in his cabin, standing at the high table, the lantern burning overhead and a chart of the coast he made on his previous trip spread out before him.

Beside the chart lay his ebony protractor, which apparently he had been using to plot the ship's course southward. I was surprised to see it there for during the whole of the voyage, from Nantucket to Magdalena Bay, it had been hidden from sight. With an embarrassed look, as if I had caught him in the act of pilfering the ship's funds, he opened a drawer and put it away.

"Troll's left us," he said. " 'Twas somehow fated. Dost think the Indians will make him a god shouldst they find him floating about? No, unlike our Jeremy, he hath not the shape nor physiognomy for such a lofty role."

"We have a problem," I said. "The ship lacks a captain. Jim Blanton is next in line . . ."

"Blanton!" Caleb broke in, giving me the impression that he had never heard of the first mate before. "The tall, hungry-looking one or the round one of well-fed mien?"

"Neither," I replied. "Blanton's bald and wears a beard."

"I've glimpsed him. What thinkest thou, Nathan, wouldst make us a proper captain? Doth he know the ship's pointed end from the blunt end? Canst scan a sail and read the wind and limn the lurking shoal?"

I hesitated with my answer, overcome because never before had he asked me a question of importance.

"Speak up," Caleb said. "Thou hast seen a goodly part of the watery world. Thou hast seen men stand before their God and lie. Thou hast seen men die ignobly. Thou hast found a wondrous treasure in the sea. Unloose thy tongue, therefore. Thoughts unsaid clutter the mind and do in time make it bilious. What dost think of Blanton? Doth his manly beard conceal a coward?"

Emboldened, I said, "From what I've seen of him Blanton would be a bad choice. He knows the ship but little about navigation. When there was talk of mutiny he and Troll were always the ringleaders. Also, the only man in the crew who likes him is the cook."

"How doth Tom Waite strike thee? He seemeth a lively fellow. Perchance too lively, since the good captains I've known are more the sober-sided kind, those given to long thoughts."

"Tom's all right," I said.

"Wouldst trust thy life to him and the life of the crew and the ship's life?"

As I thought about his question, my eyes fell upon the chart spread out on the table. The straight line of the course he was plotting when I entered the cabin showed clear.

"What say, Nathan? Dost thou wish to summon Tom Waite?"

We looked at each other across the width of the cabin.

There was no doubt at all that his question was sincere. If I had agreed upon Tom Waite as our new captain, he would have summoned him that instant, of this I am certain. But it was not the right choice and I did not make it. I took from the drawer the protractor, which Caleb had hidden, and placed it on the table beside the chart he had been working with only a few minutes before.

"Captain Clegg," I said, "what are your orders?"

150

My words sounded dramatic, overly so I suppose, for I felt embarrassed as I spoke them, and Caleb, tugging at his beard, looked away. He picked up the big white cat and put it down, walked slowly to the porthole and gazed out.

"Have the men on deck at once," he said, in a voice that now had a different sound to me. "And stir thy stumps about it. We waste precious time whilst thou stand there gawking."

22

In high spirits I ran forward along the deck to give Caleb's orders to our first mate, Mr. Blanton. He was not at the bow where I had seen him earlier or below, but I found him at last on the quarterdeck. He stood at the wheel, idly moving it back and forth, his feet squared and his cap set at a jaunty angle.

"Captain Clegg," I said, "has given the order to sail."

I spoke twice before he heard me, so lost was he in his own thoughts. For a moment his hands tightened on the wheel. Then they dropped to his sides and hung there, two great fists with which he had been known to drive a nail into a hard pine plank.

I was tempted to explain to him why he had not been chosen as our new captain, but watching the men-

acing, knotty fists that hung at his side, decided not to.
"Caleb Clegg once was captain," I said, "and is again."

"He has no right," Blanton said. "He's got no captain's papers."

"He will have them when he reaches Nantucket,"
I replied.

"He's crazy to boot," Blanton said.

"About some things," I answered, "but not about
sailing a ship."

Blanton thrust his fists behind him. I felt that he
was weighing the possibilities of mutiny, going over
them step by step in his slow mind, balancing the rewards against the consequences.

"We are more than a thousand leagues from home,"
I said. "We need an experienced captain. Without
one, none of us is safe — neither us nor the ambergris."

It was the mention of the ambergris, the casks that
were worth more than twenty thousand dollars, that
I think brought him to his senses. As he thrust his
fists into his pockets, I started for the ladderway.

"Ask your brother about the thing," he said surlily,
"the thing that's hanging to our stern. Shall I cut it
loose or hoist it?"

I was minded to tell Blanton to put the life buoy on

153

deck, but not being sure what my brother intended to do with it, I said nothing and departed.

Caleb was bent over the table with a chart spread out before him, the ebony protractor in his hand. He had taken the lantern down from its hook and it sat on a pile of books beside him, casting a strong light across the table. I saw at a glance that it was not the chart of the Pacific Coast which lay in front of him, which he had been working on before, but a new chart, one of the broad Pacific and the islands of the southern seas. Truthfully, I must say that at the moment, at the sight of it lying there, my blood ran cold.

"Hast given the order?" Caleb said, not looking up.

My answer must have come forth in a mumble, for he asked me again, "Hast given the order?"

"Blanton wants to know about the life buoy," I said. "Do you wish it hoisted aboard or left tethered at the stern?"

Caleb straightened up and glanced at me as if I as well as Blanton had lost our wits. "Aboard! Aboard! 'Tis not a kedge to tow or yet a sea anchor in a storm. 'Tis a life buoy, the dark canoe which is tethered there. Have Mr. Blanton bring it aboard and seest thou that it's lashed down securely. Who knows when we shalt need it, in what great storm or dire confrontation?"

I stumbled out of the cabin and up the ladder to the quarterdeck, where I gave my brother's orders to the waiting Blanton. On my return, finding Caleb again bent over the chart table, I quietly approached and glanced over his shoulder. He had drawn a line from Magdalena Bay to the southernmost of the Hawaiian Islands and was about to draw a second line from this point southeastward to the Marquesas. It was not the course that would take the ship homeward to Nantucket.

I decided to wait no longer. I could already hear the winches at work, hoisting the life buoy on board. In less than a half an hour the anchor would be raised and the sails unfurled.

"What," I blurted out, "what's the reason for plotting a course to the South Seas?"

Caleb slowly finished the line he was drawing and laid the protractor aside. "Dost think we shall not find him there?" he said.

"Find who?" I asked.

"Thou know him well from thy reading," Caleb said. "The monstrous Moby Dick. Dost think him there or doth the devious-cruising Whale push his pleated brow through colder latitudes? Off Nippon's shores, mayhap? Where thinkest thou he now spends his crafty hours?"

Caleb's eyes were calm. And his question was spoken in a calmly, brotherly way, as if he meant to consider my answer whatever it might be.

"I think that Moby Dick is dead," I answered. "Dead many years ago."

"Thou knowest, Nathan, that ordinary whales have longer lives than mortal men. Twice as long, I've heard. And Moby Dick lives not by ordinary rules, either of beasts or man. We shall find him, I think, still in life's prime, though he may now prefer warmer, equatorial seas to those of northern climes."

"He's dead," I repeated. "If not from old age, then from a ship's harpoon."

Caleb's eyes clouded for a moment at the thought of the White Whale's death, but he said, "No, 'tis our harpoons alone he waits for."

On the deck I could hear the scurrying of feet, the preparations for departure. "Let's say that the White Whale is alive," I said, taking another tack, "and we decide to hunt him down, who will go with us? Not the crew aboard this ship. There's not a man, except Judd, who wouldn't rise up against us. Everyone is anxious to get home. Don't forget their unspent wages — the casks of ambergris — that they talk about day and night. What will be their pay for hunting Moby Dick?"

It was a strong argument I gave him in this warning, since I spoke the hard truth, yet he passed it over with a shrug.

157

"They'll do what I command," he said. "Did not Ahab's men follow him?"

"Yes, to their death, but you are not Ahab and this is not his crew," I said. "Listen, Caleb. You've found the *Amy Foster,* after a search which few men would

have the courage to make. You've brought up a fortune in ambergris. And most important of all, you
now have the logbook. It lies there in front of you.
We are taking it to Nantucket. The board of inquiry
will see that you were right and Jeremy was wrong."

Caleb was listening to what I said, yet deep behind
his gaze I saw the lurking image of Moby Dick. It was
there, it had been there for all the years I remembered,
this unloved man's hatred of a world that in its indif-
ferent way had also hated him. But how in the passing of an hour do you slay the white-humped monster?

At this moment Mr. Blanton knocked at the door
and said that the tide would be turning in a quarter
hour and asked if we should wait.

"Wait!" I shouted and turned again to my brother.
"More than likely the Whale is dead," I told him.
"The crew will not obey your orders. You have found
all that you came to find."

Caleb slowly turned away from me and again began
to study the chart.

"Do you remember," I said in desperation, "at the
end of the book where Ahab has finally come upon
Moby Dick, the whale boats are wrecked and the
Parsee drowned and the ship itself is in danger from

the White Whale's fury, at that time his good friend Starbuck spoke to him. He pled with Ahab, saying . . ."

Caleb looked up. "Aye, his words I recall. 'Never, never wilt thou capture him, old man,' cried Starbuck. 'In Jesus's name no more of this, that's worse than devil's madness. Two days chased. Twice stove to splinters. Thy very leg once more snatched from under thee. Thy evil shadow gone — all good angels mobbing thee with warnings — what more wouldst thou have? Shall we be dragged by him to the bottom of the sea? Shall we be towed by him to the infernal world? Oh, oh — Impiety and blasphemy to hunt him more!' Aye, 'tis . . ."

"And there's another thing that Starbuck said," I broke in. "He said, near the end, before the ship went down with all hands, save Ishmael . . ."

"Aye, Ishmael was saved by the dark canoe."

"Starbuck cried out to Ahab, whom he loved," I went on. " 'Oh! Ahab, not too late is it, even now, the third day, to desist. See! Moby Dick seeks thee not. It is thou, thou, that madly seekest him!' "

"Aye, 'twas his good, dear friend, Starbuck, who spoke to him thus, as thou now speak to me."

Caleb left the chart table and made his way to the porthole. As he looked out toward Rehusa Strait, as the big white cat hopped to his shoulder and nestled there, he said:

> "To Mercy, Pity, Peace, and Love
> All pray in their distress. . . . .
> For Mercy, Pity, Peace, and Love
> Is God, our father dear."

I opened the cabin door and went on deck. There was nothing more that I could say.

23

ALERT SAILED promptly on a light wind and the turning tide.

Caleb was at the helm. Standing at his side, watching as he moved the big wheel and shouted a final command to the men aloft, I could not tell where we were bound, whether homeward or to the far waters of the Pacific. His eyes were shadowed beneath his heavy brows, fixed upon something that I could not see. His jaw was firmly set. There was no sign.

Under half-sail we moved down Magdalena Bay, past its stony promontories and through the shallows of Rehusa Strait.

A mile or more from the strait, as we met the first Pacific surge, Caleb asked me to call the crew to the quarterdeck. When the men were gathered around him, he ordered the life buoy lowered. Mr. Blanton gladly swung the davits, for the buoy was dripping water on his freshly swabbed deck. It met the sea and as the men who unloosed it scrambled back, the buoy trailed out astern, held by a stout line.

Caleb handed the wheel to me. He then drew a knife from his belt, limped to the rail, and with one swift stroke cut the line that held the buoy fast.

Twisting in the breeze, the freed line dropped away. The buoy rolled and righted itself and at last settled down upon the gentle sea. Caleb watched it fall astern, until it was but a speck to my straining eyes, before he looked around at us and spoke.

"The dark canoe," he said, "moveth with the wind and the waves and the moon's constant tides. It moveth at its own pace, slower by far than this stout bark which bears us homeward. Yet in time it will outpace our many sails and make ports that we shall never see."

The sun had reached the horizon and for a moment or two floated there, casting a bright glow across the deck, upon all our faces. Caleb glanced at each of us in turn.

"Dost thou doubt me, Mr. Blanton?" he said. "Dost think that thou canst hold the wind in thy hand and cup the surging wave and snare the speeding moon?

Dost believe, Tom Waite, only that which thou canst put in thy mouth and chew upon, which thou canst touch with thy finger? There's more to things than that. Aye, more!"

Blanton coughed. Tom Waite turned his eyes from Caleb and winked at me. Falling silent, Caleb hobbled to the rail. In the descending dusk, the men drifted away one by one, except for Old Man Judd. When they were gone my brother came and looked down at the compass.

"Thy course," he said to me, "ranges south by southeast. Hold steady and mind the sails. Watch the ship's white wake. It will tell thee where thou hast been and where thou goest."

With a last glance astern, he left us. Thin light still lingered overhead. I turned to look for the dark canoe. It was gone.

Judd said, "This book you've been reading, I forget its name . . ."

"*Moby-Dick.*"

"Sometime I'd like to look at it."

"You can have it now," I said. "It's on my bunk."

Rehusa Strait was black against the sky. Beyond it stood the peaks of Isla Ballena. I regretted that we could not take Jeremy back to Nantucket and bury him among the elms. But if one must die, I thought, what better place to be than on a windy headland where sea-birds nest and you are worshiped as a god.

Our sails held the wind. The light shining on the compass rose showed that the course was homeward, the course that Caleb and I, the two of us, had laid out together. The night wind freshened and fair Antares glowed in the west.

165

9181

F   O'Dell, Scott.
ODE

      The dark canoe.